The Friggin' Altos

A Crime Family Gone Crazy

By

LaVerne and Sam Zocco

© 2002 by LaVerne and Sam Zocco.
All rights reserved.

No part of this book may be reproduced, stored in a retrieval system, or transmitted by any means, electronic, mechanical, photocopying, recording, or otherwise, without written permission from the author.

ISBN: 0-7596-7249-0

This book is printed on acid free paper.

1stBooks - rev. 3/11/02

ACKNOWLEDGEMENTS

To my husband, John L. Zocco, who came from a wonderful, happy Sicilian family who used to make me laugh so hard I cried with stories of the mafia and the old country.

To my father who taught me everything I know about how wonderful Italians' are in their loyalty, their love for food and wine, and their fierce caring for their heritage. They would be the first ones to laugh at The Friggin' Altos and Love it as the spoof it is.

To our big Sicilian family in Cleveland, Ohio: this one's for you.

The Friggin' Altos
A Crime Family Gone Crazy

CHAPTER ONE

Hi, I'm Vinnie Alto. Maybe you've heard of me.

I used to be a big-shot crime boss in the Bronx in New York. Then I moved the family to Florida and we all went insane, one way or another.

If you're thinking I'm one of the old Dons from books and movies, forgetaboutit. I may be rough around the edges when it comes to manners, or English grammar, but I ain't like John Gotti whose imprisonment was the death of the old Mafia. He was from the old school of whack everybody in sight. He gave the FBI the chance to catch him dead to rights with their electronic wiretaps and fucken microphones planted in stoolies' hats. No, those days are long gone and I say good riddance.

Today whether you realize it or not, my whole empire is right there on the internet in front of your eyes if you got a PC and a brain. I got several web-sites selling bogus stocks, touting scam operations, and sending coded messages to my global companies run by real savvy accountants. I got a cell phone, a psychiatrist, a Lear Jet and a swanky office in Midtown Manhattan. I also got a Russian mob member for my lawyer, and a public relation firm on Fifth Avenue that keeps my image pure and squeaky clean.

Sure I'm Sicilian but there is only one code from the old mobs I believe in and that's family honor. Most of the old rules have dropped by the wayside in this new age. There is no more "Omerta," or code of silence. Today every trusted low life is spilling his guts on the internet to make money, write a book, or save his skin from indictment. In that atmosphere you can't and don't trust anyone. However in a very important way I'm different from all the other crime bosses and this difference has caused my downfall.

You see, every member of my inner circle are family members, relatives, and every one of them is an idiot. I'm trying to run a contemporary and with-it operation, and my closest associates are operating like the three stooges. It's one of the reasons I decided to move this family of nincompoops to Florida. I thought I could control these screw-ups better if I could find a more peaceful and slower life where I wouldn't have to worry about them fucking up every time I turned around and where the chances for major problems could be kept to a minimum. Down among the palms and tropical breezes things would be simpler, a small operation would be doable, and I could keep this tiny group separate from my real empire. I could play Don to "The Friggin Altos," for laughs.

There were other considerations too. I had a wonderful wife named Rose and two bratty children named Carmella, the apple of my eye, and Little Vinnie, the sulking prince. The nucleus of my family operation compared to my world-wide empire were my cousins, Ricco, Sammy Six Toes, Pete and Santo. My enforcer was a kid I picked up off the streets named Frankie. Rose and I made him an honorary member of the Alto family years ago. Trotsky, my lawyer, was a childhood friend and was also included in our family.

So you see there were just ten of us compared to thousands of employees who worked in my global enterprises. So why couldn't I keep these ten in line? It is a mystery and an enigma. I'm sure it had something to do with genes, lust and insanity.

In my schizophrenic world it fell on my shoulders to deal with problems and threats in a civilized way. In a world of amazing technology you could do a lot to amass huge amounts of money or create more wealth, but it couldn't help you deal with traitors, rats and human nature. Human nature was unpredictable and unknowable.

People are not computers and their emotions run high and wide.

It was easy to hide money all over the world in numbered Bank Accounts and not pay taxes on anything. It was easy to scam the stock market, build legitimate businesses and live like a king. It was not easy to hide a slightly pregnant girlfriend from my wife, deal with a partner who betrayed me, or cope with a childhood friend who was out to kill me. I knew I needed help with these problems and that's why I finally went to a psychiatrist.

In this new world we have you can handle wealth, you just can't handle people. It's just the opposite from the old mob days when people followed orders but huge wealth eluded you.

By the time I turned forty, I was wealthy beyond anything you can imagine. I was a big shot crime boss but it hadn't always been that way. For me it was a lot of hard work, and the rest was blind luck. I came to understand that the old ways were ancient and I knew I had to keep up with the new times or I would be history. The world had changed into this technological wonder that turned doing mob business, like murder, loan sharking, prostitution and gambling into dinosaurs.

The Friggin' Altos
A Crime Family Gone Crazy

Other bosses, like my old nemesis, Jimmy Pecan, a real psycho of a crumb, didn't seem to have the trouble I was having. Jimmy, he was always suave and elegant, but whacko, you know.

He and I grew up together, and it was Jimmy who shot me in the ass over some dame both of us forgot a long time ago. I'm not kidding. The bullet lodged in my lower back right where the moon shines when you take your pants down. I got my reasons for mentioning this very unpleasant subject, and for why I have never forgiven Jimmy for sneaking up on me when I had the broad down on the ground in the alley ready to pop my cookies.

Anyway, everybody in the whole friggin' town was scared shitless of this moron, but he seemed to lead a charmed life, like he had a pact or something with the devil.

His organization just grew and grew, while mine seemed to languish. I tried to figure out why that was. The answer to that question was pretty easy to pinpoint. I wasn't living in the contemporary modern world. I was still trudging along with old fashioned ideas that were getting me nowhere. That's when I decided to get in step with the universe and modernize my operation. I hired some shady consulting and investment firms, parted with some of my hard-earned profits and it worked like a charm. From there the whole thing took off, the money came rolling in, and I was at the top of my game. Some of the old operations I left alone like my cheese factory in Jersey. It was small but it was profitable, so much so, I kept two sets of books.

Pecan, on the other hand, was still using old mob tactics, but for him they seemed to work. He was whacking everyone who got in his way and he kept his boys happy, loyal and contented.

Things got so good for me I finally decided to move to Florida. My ex-partner, Tony Sweets, was satisfied with his buy-out share of the cheese factory, and I had talked my slightly pregnant girlfriend, Lacy Love, into accepting a nice bank account in exchange for her silence that our affair would never reach my wife Rose's delicate ears. Rose was patient and loving, but the one thing she prized above all was my faithfulness. It was the one thing I couldn't give her.

So where did it all start to go so terribly wrong for me?

I can tell you the very minute, date and year. It was the day I was at my shrink, Dr. Ruth. It was December and close to Christmas, just one year ago. I remember dismissing Frankie with the

The Friggin' Altos
A Crime Family Gone Crazy

Lexus and walking over to the medical building on Fifth Avenue. I hadn't been sleeping well lately, and though I knew the source of my anxiety very well, I was giving the doc the old who-haw.

Don't let the name fool you, Dr. Ruth was a looker and she gave me a woody every time I walked into her office and smelled her perfume. She was trying her best to worm my feelings out of me, being all sensitive and that shit, when my cell phone rang.

"Excuse me doll, I got to get this. It's important." She sat back with those long legs stretched out a mile and sucked on a pencil. Could you just die? I know I could. She was a babe.

"Yeah, Yeah, what?"

It was Frankie.

"We found Tony Sweets." He announced it like he had just been signed by the Yankees to play in the World Series.

"Where'd you find the rat?"

"He was hiding in his old Lady's condo. Me and the boys took him over to the Diamond Wheel." The Diamond Wheel is my nightclub and strip joint I own.

"How come he didn't skip town when he had the chance?"

Frankie sounded disbelieving. "Do you believe he and the Feds crossed communication wires. They got the search warrant early and didn't give him enough time to get gone. You want me to get Brutto Demenza to take care of this?"

"Naw, we only use Brutto for the big jobs."

Frankie breathed a sigh of relief.

"Thank God. That guy gives me the fucken chills. So what do you want us to do?"

"Just keep him tied up at the club. We'll let him sweat for a couple of days. Get a hold of Pete and Santo on the cell phone and tell them they got a job to do. Then go down to the courthouse and get my mother. Pay her fine and drive her home."

"What the hell she do this time?"

It was my turn to be exasperated. "She drove her ranger through Bloomingdale's window."

"Soused again?"

"What else. Since Pop died she's getting to be a handful. Maybe the move to Florida will straighten her out."

"We still moving down there?"

"As soon as Trotsky sells the properties and we tie up loose ends we're shaking the dust of this town off our shoes. Oh, by the way, I know it's asking a lot, but could you pick up Carmella from the orthodontist?"

The Friggin' Altos
A Crime Family Gone Crazy

He sounded so unhappy. "Do I have to? She's such a pain in the ass. Her and her little school chums."

"Hey, she's your goddaughter. Seventeen-year-olds are supposed to be pains. Please do it for Rose."

I could always wheedle him into anything.

He laughed his warm laugh. He was the handsomest guy I ever set eyes on. "For Rose, I'll do it."

"Thanks. You know Frankie, Carmella is the last of my kids. She's my little girl. When I think of any scumbag boy putting their hands on her, I want to cry. I want her to stay at home forever. She's so innocent, so pure, so—"

"Jeez Vinnie, stop. You'll have me blubbering in a minute."

"Okay, okay. I'll see you back at the Mansion this evening."

I hung up the phone and looked over at the doc.

"You know, Vinnie, you shouldn't be discussing murder in my office. It's not covered by confidentiality."

I laughed. She was a pretty bright broad.

"How would you like to move down to Florida? Wouldn't you like to take a shot at paradise?"

"You've been talking about moving for a while now. When is all this going to happen?"

I got up and moved over so I was standing over her. I gave her my sexy intense look.

"Never mind when. I leave all those kinds of details to Trotsky, my lawyer. Well, what do you say? I'll set you up in an office, pay you two hundred thou a year, and get you a nice house on the ocean. See, I think I'm going to need you to get me through some situations that are coming up."

"You want me to raise your dosage of medication?"

I reached down and groped her breast a little. Just a friendly gesture to seal the bargain.

"I don't want nothing but you say yes."

She laughed with her whole body.

"Okay, I'll think it over. It's taken me a long time to build up my business here. But, I think you just made me an offer—"

"Yeah, yeah, I know the rest. Now, I gotta go. You understand, of course, I wasn't discussing any murder over the phone. You been seeing too many mob movies on TV. I'll see you at my regular time next week. Trotsky will get in touch with you with the details."

The Friggin' Altos
A Crime Family Gone Crazy

God, I wanted to climb all over that woman. It was an iffy go because I really couldn't read her too well yet. Usually a man has a sense of will she or won't she, but she was totally neutral on the subject. I thought at the time, there's always time. That shows how much I knew.

Anyway, I left the office with some samples of sleeping pills. I know I was busy thinking about Tony Sweets, my partner, who was going to be my guest for a while. Now, I know there was a lot going on that I knew nothing about. I can tell you now that it all played itself out, but remember, at the time I was ignorant of all these little side trips. I think one of the reasons I went to the shrink in the first place was because I was sensing things around me were not right. Everybody seemed to be acting okay, on the surface, but I was floating around in a sea of deception that was making me very anxious and depressed.

I can tell you the major thing that was causing these feelings had to do with me and not with anyone in my environment. It just so happened that a few days earlier, I learned from my doctor that the old bullet that Jimmy pumped into me had loosened up from where it had been concrete all these years. You know you can live with a bullet all your life so long as it stays put, but if it starts to travel in your system you're a goner. I knew from the look on the doctor's face that it was bad news. For now the bullet was loose, but if it started traveling, it would go straight for my heart. When it hit I would die. So you can see that was one thing that was filling my head so much, I wasn't looking at what was going on around me. If you go on to the next chapter you'll know what I didn't know. When I think of looking at it from your point of view, I guess it was kind of funny. To tell you the truth, it was hilarious. But, you judge for yourself.

The fact I wrote this book is no ghostly thing. What you're reading comes from my diaries I secretly kept on my computer. Rose, my wife, found them by accident and took the disks to a publisher. I just wanted you to know that.

The Friggin' Altos
A Crime Family Gone Crazy

CHAPTER TWO

Okay, you made it through Chapter One. So now you know I'm your guide and storyteller for the duration, and even though I find some of these things hurtful, I wouldn't be doing my job if I didn't explain as we went along how things affected me. You might find me repeating some things cause I want you to be sure and understand exactly what was happening to me. It ain't every crime boss that writes a book, so this is a wonderful opportunity to see what makes us tick. Actually, it's a wonderful opportunity for me to toot my horn and let you peek in at a crime family gone insane.

You know I was depressed enough to see a psychiatrist. I learned an old bullet I was carrying around inside me had started to loosen up from where it was buried in my back. If the bullet shifted a little, then it wouldn't have mattered so much, but the doctor said, when he showed me the little bugger on the x-ray, that it was not only loose, it was starting to move out into my system. It could travel slow or fast, but once it hit my heart I would die instantly. The whole idea was driving me crazy.

LaVerne and Sam Zocco

Besides the bullet, I was dealing with my nutty mother, Frances, who was a drunk. And I also had a pregnant girlfriend Lacy I was about to leave because I was moving the family to Florida. Oh, yeah, I told you about them.

Anyway, here's the scene that was going on while I was having dinner with my wife Rose at the Alto Mansion on the day the boys rousted out Tony Sweets from behind his mother's skirts in her condo. Tony Sweets, my ex-partner rat, was waiting for me to show up at the Diamond Wheel, my club and strip-joint in midtown New York. He was all tied up if you get my meaning. But this scene didn't involve Tony Sweets. I learned a long time after about all of this. It involved my beloved enforcer Frankie after he picked up my seventeen-year-old daughter, Carmella, from the orthodontist. This is word for word what he told me with some running commentary of my own.

"Get your freaking hands off my zipper. Now sit back in your seat and try to behave like a lady." Frankie my enforcer braked the car to a complete stop.

"How come you don't like me Frankie? When I was a little girl you couldn't wait to hold me?" My daughter Carmella Alto, long of leg, large of

The Friggin' Altos
A Crime Family Gone Crazy

breast, and filthy of mouth, I learned to my chagrin. She straightened up in frustration.

Frankie zipped himself up and turned to look over at my girl who had tears in her eyes and pouted staring straight ahead through the windshield. He wanted to feel sorry for her, but he couldn't lower his defenses with this dark eyed, raven hair beauty. Hey, that's what he said. She had a body that wouldn't quit, and he knew if he allowed himself to even think for a second what she would feel like in his arms, he would be dead. Maybe he wouldn't mind dying for her if her father was anyone else but me. But, it had been me who had saved him from a life of crime and poverty. When the head of a crime family takes you in, the Sicilian Code expects loyalty at all times. That means you don't bad rap the boss, you don't squeal, you do as you're told and what you're told, and you don't screw the daughter.

Frankie banged on the steering wheel in anger.

"Look, Carmella, you're still a little girl, and you're Vinnie's little girl. Oh, don't cry. Listen to me. I love your father. I want to tell you, it isn't that you're not attractive, even a knockout. But, there can never be anything between us, you spoiled little brat, so get that through your head. Now come on. Behave yourself."

LaVerne and Sam Zocco

She wouldn't be my daughter if she weren't stubborn.

She turned to look into Frankie's tan eyes with all the intensity she could muster.

"Johnnie Mizner stuck his tongue down my throat yesterday, and I let him put his hand up my dress. I'll bet I'm the only virgin left at St. Agnes." She was a little minx all right—really a hell cat when she wanted her own way.

Frankie couldn't help but mutter an, "Oh God."

Oh, she wasn't going to let him off that easy.

Carmella grabbed his hand and pulled it toward her.

"Look, Frankie, you ever seen breasts as firm as these? And just run your hand up my leg. Hey, where you going?"

Well, Frankie couldn't take it another minute. He jumped out of the car and slammed the door. He stuck his head in through the window.

"I'm walking the rest of the way. Tell your father I wasn't feeling so good." He turned away and took a few steps in the street.

Carmella slid over to the driver's side and yelled after him, "Coward."

And Frankie, being the sensible man I always thought he was shouted back, "Yeah, but a live coward."

The Friggin' Altos
A Crime Family Gone Crazy

So there you have it. Completely unbeknownst to me, her father, as well as her mother, Carmella was trying to seduce my enforcer and wasn't having any luck.

Maybe you think I'm too protective of my daughter, or that my eyes are easy to pull the wool over, but the truth is I love my daughter so much I could never envision that she was a slut. Me, being the boss, who was going to tell me different? Rose my wife had more than an inkling that Carmella was not the sweet nun I made her out to be, but she wasn't going to try to convince me of that. Rose is a wise woman in her way. She thinks the things you learn for yourself are the things that you believe, so she was willing to keep me in the dark about Carmella until it was revealed right in front of me. Then I would have to believe it. In my own mind, I was in the dark when I shouldn't have been. Had I been any kind of reasonable person when it came to Carmella, Frankie would never have had to suffer as he did. He would have been able to come to me like a man and tell me what was going on. I guess I actually thought, since there was such an age difference between them, maybe seven years, it would make a difference in what Frankie was feeling. How stupid could I be? Tell me the truth, you twenty-four-year-old men out there, what would you be doing if a seventeen-year-old was coming on to you? When I think about it in those terms, I got to give Frankie admiration for his determination, and maybe an "F" for stupidity.

But see, I wasn't seeing Carmella like a beautiful young woman, I could only see her as my daughter. I thought I knew that Frankie would never pull anything because it would mean certain death to him, and that knowledge would keep him clean.

Well, this day it was. There would be other days down the line, but on this particular day Frankie was thinking good sense even when being bombarded by the temptation to end all temptations. For this one day, he fought the devil, and Frankie won.

So there I am at the dinner table completely ignorant that any of this was going on. At the same time there was a scene going on between Tony Sweets and my enforcers, Ricco and Sammy Six Toes down at the Diamond Wheel.

My lawyer, Ivan Trotsky, was in the process of selling all my properties before we left for Florida. The Diamond Wheel Club had already been sold to the City Social Service Agency, and was going to be renovated into a shelter for the homeless.

The Friggin' Altos
A Crime Family Gone Crazy

When they brought Tony in he was sweating like a pig. Him and those goofy snakeskin shoes he always wore. Tony liked to think of himself as another Jimmy Walker, the dapper former Mayor of New York, who dressed like a fashion plate, and had the personality of a beloved major movie star. Yeah, that was Tony all right. But Tony had no patience. His stupid temper always got him in trouble, even when we were kids. He was a hot head who never wanted to listen to the other guy. He had a one way view about everything, the Tony view, and he got rid of anyone who disagreed with him.

Now, you can't have a member of your gang bumping guys off right and left. In the case of Angelo Tutti, he and Tony got into some freakin' argument and Tony guns him down. This time he made a big mistake. He took the corpse over the State line to bury it and got picked up by federal agents.

It was kind of funny. There was Tony with a shovel digging a hole out in nowhere, with Angelo in the trunk, when these guys come along and ask if they can help. It's my understanding that Angelo wasn't quite dead enough at that minute though he died before they got the trunk up. There was pounding, and moaning, and before it was all over they had Tony in a cell.

Tony gave them some razzle-dazzle about self-defense, but they weren't buying. And that would have been the end of Tony into the Federal system, if he hadn't opened his mouth and ratted me, his partner and childhood friend, out to the Brooks Brothers, our name for Federal Agents at the time.

He told them me and the boys were cooking the books at the Alto Cheese Factory, that there were two sets, ones that the IRS got, and the real ones. The suits, another name for the federal agents, got hot to trot with that information and offered Tony a way out of his misfortune. If he told them where they could find the books, they would get a warrant, give Tony two days to get out of town, then come down on "The Friggin' Altos," as they liked to call us, harder than a gay rights activist.

In a way I can't blame Tony. He didn't want to be buried for the rest of his life in prison and never again see the light of day, so he fucked me over. I can understand that. I can't forgive it, but I can understand it.

It just so happened that the lying Federales got the warrant one day early and never gave Tony time to hit the pavement and get out of town. They presented themselves at the Alto Cheese Factory

The Friggin' Altos
A Crime Family Gone Crazy

with warrant in hand, however, my lawyer, Trotsky, was there and found enough loopholes in the warrant they thought they were toting Swiss cheese. The poor suits had to go all the way back to Manhattan, The Cheese factory being out in Jersey, to find another Federal judge who wasn't on our payroll and get another signed warrant. By that time the books were long gone. All they found were the substitute books and a grinning Trotsky.

That meant Tony was clear of the FBI agents, but he wasn't worrying about them. Being a man of exquisite taste he knew his elegant little body was a goner. He ran wailing and praying to his mother's condo and hid up in her crawlspace. Three hours later the boys brought him into the club, shaking and crying, then as quiet as he could be. They took him to the cellar and tied him up to one of the chairs.

Tony, being a pragmatist could see he was all out of luck. "Hey Ricco," he pleaded, "how about a Perrier?" Didn't I tell you he was elegant? Perrier! What a helluva guy.

Ricco looks at him with dismay, cause Ricco, though he made his bones early, around fifteen, killing some poor schnook of a union member that couldn't keep his mouth shut about where the pension monies were going during open meetings, was a compassionate guy and he liked Tony Sweets.

"Sorry, Tony, orders from Vinnie. Nothing to drink. You can have a smoke though."

"Naw, I'm wearing the patch. When's Vinnie coming?"

See he was sweating and worried all the time, but he didn't want to look like no blubbering baby.

Ricco saw through his bravado.

"Don't be so nervous. He'll be here when he gets here. Nice shoes Tony. What the hell they made out of?"

Now I know that made Tony feel more relaxed cause he laughed. That's what Ricco told me.

"Snakeskin. You like them?"

"Are you kidding. My kid would kill me if he saw me wearing animal skin, even reptile. He's big on animal rights. Made me go down to the pound and adopt "Meatball," the cat."

Then Tony turns to Six Toes. See, Six Toes ain't as compassionate as Ricco. He hates a rat.

"What time is it, Six Toes?"

Sammy's really going to rub it into Sweets.

"Almost midnight. Why, you going somewheres?"

Tony ain't as relaxed as before.

The Friggin' Altos
A Crime Family Gone Crazy

"Guess I'm in really deep merda, right?" For those who ain't Italian merda means shit.

What a question to ask Six Toes when Sweets nearly had us in prison forever.

"Naw, how can you say that?" Six Toes was being sarcastic here if you didn't get that. "All you did was tell the Feds the books for the Alto Cheese Company were cooked. And then you run away and hide out in your poor mother's condo. You're a piece of turd, Tony."

Then everything stops when they hear our footsteps coming down the hall.

Tony all but squeaks now. "What's that."

And Sammy Six Toes slams home the last coffin nail.

"Those are the sounds of death, you friggin stoolie. I can hardly wait."

Then Frankie and I make our entrance after making arrangements to go play some cards over at The White Palace for an alibi later on in the week. And after Frankie contacted Pete and Santo on their cell phone, our torpedoes, that they had a job to do a couple of days down the line taking care of Tony Sweets.

I remember Frankie asking me if I was going to use Brutto Demenza for the job. Of course I told him we only used Brutto for the big jobs. He said he was glad cause Brutto gave him the freakin chills. To tell you the truth, I always prayed the job would never be so big we had to get Demenza. So far it had worked.

Frankie gave the cousins the secret phrase to tell me Tony Sweets was dead. When the job was done, they would call me at home to tell me.

That was the last I ever saw of Tony Sweets alive.

The Friggin' Altos
A Crime Family Gone Crazy

CHAPTER THREE

Let's see where were we. Oh, yeah. The night Tony Sweets was whacked by my cousins, Pete and Santo, I was in the kitchen by myself having a glass of wine thinking about when we was kids. It was late and I was feeling very depressed. It's never easy to order a murder: it takes a lot out of you. For me, I knew I was looking forward to weird nightmares and more sleeping pills. But what could I do. You got to keep the organization clear of squealers and rats.

I mentioned I was having dinner with Rose when all of this was going on. I think this would be a good time to tell you about Rose and me, what we look like, things like that. You have to forgive me but I'm new to this writing game. Anyway, when most non-Italians think of Italian women they think of dark hair and dark eyes and pretty when the girls are young. But aging takes its toll and they end up fat, sloppy and having mustaches. That's true of some, but not of my Rose. She's blond, willowy and tall. Her ancestors came from the North of Italy near the Swiss border around Albania. She must have some Swiss blood in the family because her whole family has the light hair and light eyes.

Me, I'm Sicilian through and through. Average height, average weight, a little more now that I just passed my fortieth birthday. I do have the dark brown eyes and dark brown wavy hair of my "paisanos" but Rose tells me I got a handsome face.

In case you're wondering, Rose and I met in the neighborhood when we were about seventeen. She was working hard trying to get through school, and working for my lawyer Trotsky's mother in the afternoons. Me I was hanging and dealing.

Trotsky was a good kid then and we used to hang around together along with Jimmy Pecan and Ricco and Six Toes. He would often have us over to his house when suppertime came. Most of our parents were hard working people who let you kind of shift for yourself. It was all right with us, we found plenty of things to do like skipping school, giving the broads the eye, and committing little acts of petty larceny. Most afternoons we would stand outside the Don's restaurant and admire his shiny car. But not Ivan Trotsky and not Rose. They both had dreams. Ivan knew he was going to be a lawyer from the time he could say his first words and pound on the table. Rose she wanted to work with kids. She was going to go into Manhattan to a fancy school to become a social worker. That is until that fateful afternoon at Trotsky's house. The first time I saw her I hate to tell you what thoughts passed through my head. I wanted her; it was that plain and simple. She thought I was a hoodlum and would have nothing to do with me. That afternoon, Jimmy, Ricco, Six Toes and me were over for another supper at the expense of the Trotsky family. They were loaded with money, yet they choose to live in an ethnic neighborhood. Damn nice people and so down to earth. They would set us up on the enclosed porch at the back of the house and the maid would serve us dinner like we was ritzy guests. Ivan was a really handsome guy, tall, dark but shy around women.

Anyway who comes out to serve us is this vision straight from heaven. I take one look at her and I can't hear or speak no more. I regressed to a bumbling, stuttering punk as I watched her every move. I think I was aware that all the other guys at the table felt the same, but I knew none of them were thunderstruck like me.

After dinner I follow her around like a little dog finally finding my tongue and rattling off like a big shot. I ask her casually for a date, and she freezes me right out. I sense that my efforts are not a complete waste, cause I see in her blue eyes that there's a spark of amusement and interest. Only she tells me she don't date good for nothings. She's heard about me and my gang but it don't cut any ice with her. She says I'm going nowhere and she doesn't have time for bums. This makes me want her all the more. Right then and there I start making plans to win her over.

I ain't the most sentimental guy in the world, but I start with phone calls. I get the number from Ivan and just to show you how serious I am about this girl, I don't let the guys listen in. She wasn't above talking to me on the phone because I can be a pretty persuasive guy when I want to be. But, I don't rush her for a date or nothing. We talk about the neighborhood, about her life, about her dreams, about her new school. See, I keep it centered right on her. I never mentioned my life, my dreams or my new school because I didn't have any. But little by little I can feel she's relaxing and that we're becoming friends. Then I really turn on the Alto charm. I start sending her flowers, but only little dollar bunches of wild flowers. I read in a book someplace from school how this lovely maiden loved wildflowers. Then I start soliciting her opinion about what I should do with my life

The Friggin' Altos
A Crime Family Gone Crazy

and how to go about it. I already knew what Vinnie Alto was going to do with his life, but it made her a part of it just to ask her opinion. After several weeks, I told her she was right, that I was nothing and would always be nothing if I didn't get serious about school and work. So I enroll in night school. That telephone call did it. I made her so excited that she allowed me to come over and show her my course schedule.

From there on it was smooth sailing. She helped me with my homework and I talked to her about what the future would be. I had enrolled in a course that had something to do with kids and she just gushed all over me.

Our first date was out on the Island at an open-air pavilion where we danced under a silver glitter ball, and walked under the stars. From there it was into the backseat of my borrowed car and Rose was mine. The next day I withdrew from all my classes. Hey, once you got something nailed, it's too late for regrets.

Oh, she sulked and fretted for a while, but then she knew she was as hooked on me as I was on her. She finally gave in and let me do the driving. It took me five more years to get on the bottom rung of the ladder I was climbing, but the day the Don was driving a less shiny, less big car than

Vinnie Alto, is the day I proposed. In a month we were settled and Rose was pregnant.

To this day she's a quiet one. I know there's a lot of thoughts whirling around in that head of hers, but she never reveals too much. In that way she's a lot like me. I also know that as long as she thinks I'm faithful everything will remain smooth as glass. But the day she finds out about the broads, strippers and Lacy, is the day my life ain't worth a nickel.

So why do I do it you're going to ask? To tell you the truth I don't know why. Maybe because I'm exposed to it all. Maybe it's to prove what a big man I am. Maybe it's cause deep down inside I don't think I really deserve Rose and my family. Maybe it's because I'm dying and I don't know when. Take your pick—they're all insane reasons but at the core every man is insane in one way or another. So I go to a shrink. A good looking one too, but all the who-haw I mouth about being so sexy and wanting to show it, is just a cover-up to keep my shrink off balance. If she ever gets down to the real Vinnie Alto, she might run out the door screaming because she's had a look into hell.

Well, there I am sitting at the kitchen table. It's about midnight and in comes my son, Little Vinnie. While Carmella, my daughter is all her

The Friggin' Altos
A Crime Family Gone Crazy

daddy; Little Vinnie is all his mother. He's tall, on the fair side, and a number one moron. He dropped out of school in the 10th grade and spends all his time acting the big shot cause he's a mob son. He loves the life. If I would let him he'd be my right-hand-man instead of Frankie. He loves blood and guts and mayhem. He ain't got a clue about life, and I know personally I'm going to be stuck with him for the rest of his life. He thinks he's going to be the next boss. For an example, he's got a good friend Crayton Hooks that lives down the block. This black kid is going to be graduating Harvard Law School in June. Personally, I think its all Affirmative Action, but what the hell if you don't grab with both hands in this world you're going to get left behind selling pencils.

Crayton comes from a good family and there has been a cord of affection between him and Little Vinnie since they met. Two personalities couldn't be so different, and yet, there's a love there that I admire. Now, when I ask Little Vinnie what he's going to be doing in June when Crayton is graduating, Little Vinnie says he's going to be down in Florida with me tooling the broads, driving flashy cars and expecting a place on my board of directors. The kids a total airhead. But then I think of Rose and how smart she is and how quiet she is about all the brains she's got, and I think maybe Little Vinnie likes to give me the old who-haw because deep down he don't think much of me as a dad. It can't be all gravy to not be able to tell the truth about what your father does for a living. For Little Vinnie It's got to be heady-stuff to have all the money you want, live the high life, and do as you please. But on the other hand when Little Vinnie sits down and thinks about where all that money and power is coming from, it may cause him to be schizophrenic about his values. Murder, extortion, taking pennies from the little guy by force, and corrupting public officials may have worked in the old days, but today he knows it all comes from the internet scams that Trotsky has masterminded and that bilk millions of people out of their hard earned cash. If you can't take pride in your family, you got nothing. The Alto Cheese Factory is just the front for a billion dollar conglomerate and its books are still cooked cause criminals can't help themselves. If they come near anything they will twist it to give them the advantage. Of course, in this Internet world of business, there are still people to corrupt and some to get rid of but my operation don't get involved with that. It's no longer a one-gang operation, this thing goes around the world and the players are assigned their jobs and they do them. I'm what you might call an entrepreneur. I find the next big opportunities and Trotsky fleshes out the possibilities and the methods to get it done. If Ivan says it's a go, it's a go. He ain't been wrong yet. So see, I'm torn between these two worlds. On the one hand I still maintain a gang to carry out my personal orders, but on the other hand I'm part of an operation so big, the United States Government can't control it. It's tentacles spread out all over the world, and when you talk about global world order, the syndicate already has it with a global crime order that is so interlocked nothing but the end of the world will be able to destroy it.

Can Little Vinnie sit down with his friends and confide that big picture? No. So he crows about the little picture, about Ricco and Six toes, my capos, about my power in the neighborhood, about small operations that he knows about that are kind of harmless, about Pete and Santo, the torpedoes, that he thinks have the greatest jobs in the world to whack people, but he's got to be humiliated deep down inside that his father ain't a banker, or a teacher, or a lawyer or doctor. He has to be content knowing his father is a thug so he acts like he don't care about nothing, doesn't do anything,

LaVerne and Sam Zocco

and doesn't know anything. It's his way of getting back at me, being the biggest disappointment in my life. If there is one thing Italian men prize it's their sons, and so long as Little Vinnie can't be proud of me, he's made it so I can't be proud of him either. It's a standoff.

"Where you been, Little Vinnie." I don't want him to think I'm sitting there so late, drinking wine, cause I'm waiting for Pete and Santo to call me with the secret sentence that will let me know Tony Sweets has been whacked.

"Crayton and I had a pick-up game, then we went for a cruise in the car and stopped and had a couple of beers."

Before I can really tell him how I feel that Crayton is graduating and he's not, the phone rings.

"Get that will you, Vin, I'm feeling tired."

He gives me a strange look but he does what he's told.

He comes back with a knowing look on his face.

"That was Santo. He told me to tell you that Al Pacino is out of the picture. What's that about?"

I laugh and try to make it sound real. "It's about a new movie that Al Pacino was supposed to make."

The Friggin' Altos
A Crime Family Gone Crazy

Little Vinnie laughs his goofy laugh.

"You mean that old guy that was in "Scent of a Woman?" He was the one that kept saying "ow ha," and drove around blind.

"Yeah, he was cool. He got the academy award for that. What's the matter dad you look tired? You're face is all gray looking."

I had to get out of there before the tears spilt down for Tony Sweets.

"It's nothing. My shrink says I'm under too much stress. I'll take a sleeping pill. I'll be fine in the morning."

"Yeah sure." He stood there while I walked past him but he didn't make any move to give me a kiss goodnight. I didn't want him to think I was weak, so I just kept going. Now, I know I should have grabbed him with both hands and kissed him and told him how sorry I was that his life would never be sane. But, I just kept walking leaving my boy behind.

CHAPTER FOUR

So Tony Sweets was dead. Him and his snakeskin shoes gone forever. Me, I was having deep meetings with Ivan to decide how we were going to cut into the three crime bosses' organizations down in Miami when we got there.

Of all the brainless schemes Ivan ever came up with was the one he sprung on me one day two weeks later at The Cheese Factory.

"Look Vinnie," he says serious like. "One of the biggest crime bosses down there is the Cuban drug king and activist, Lazaro Salsa. I've talked to him Vinnie. We been sending e-mails back and forth, in code of course, but he says he will think of letting you have a slice of the pie, if you will do one little thing for him."

Well, I'm all ears. Anytime I can add to my personal fortune I'm willing to listen. Only I knew about this Salsa guy and he owned most of the balleta racquet (the numbers game) in the whole of Florida. For him to cut in a crime boss from New York sounded a little too easy.

"Okay, I'm listening. Can't you just tell this Havana Cigar that we're coming and he's got to share? After all, this slice of the pie is peanuts to

The Friggin' Altos
A Crime Family Gone Crazy

what we make with Global Amalgamated, (our worldwide business). Why do I even bother?"

Ivan looked at me as though I was out of my mind.

"Is this Vinnie Alto I'm hearing speak these words of stupidity?"

"Hey, watch it Ivan, we may be friends but stupidity is a strong word."

"Sorry, Vinnie, but you don't seem to get it. If we get a share of the three bosses' businesses in Florida it opens up the whole South to our Global takeover, and earns us a nice piece of pocket change to boot."

"Okay, okay. I'm getting freakin' tired here. What does Salsa want in return?"

"He wants Pete and Santo to kill Castro."

I couldn't help laughing out loud.

"Is this guy fucking nuts? Castro is a dictator, it's true, but he is also the leader of a country ninety miles off our shores that our government is trying to deal with. What would happen if they found out the mob was making United States foreign policy? They'd be all over us like cheese on a burrito. The reason we get away with so much that we do illegally is because we don't cause no problems for the government. All those politicians we own up in Washington have made it quite clear. They don't mind being corrupted if it's done quietly. But, the minute the name of Vinnie Alto is mentioned out loud in any kind of a public statement, they threaten to close up shop. Without them how we going to take over the world? No, no, it's a bad idea."

"Salsa says you do this for him, and he'll smooth the way with the rest of the crime bosses. He'll make contact with Overlord Pierre of the Haitian community who does all the smuggling and extortion, and Chief Panther Bob of the Miccosukee tribe, who own all the casinos down there. Not only that, but he'll get you a liquor license from Crazy Joe, The Generalissimo of Miami."

This time I sneered.

"You telling me that I might not be able to get a fucken liquor license down there? What are they all potsa?"

"In a way, yes. You see Vinnie; Miami is a special case. It is a hotbed of activism against Castro. Not only that but all the Cubans vote the way their leaders tell them. Every candidate running for office has to make an appearance down there to make deals with the Cubans. They learn to speak Spanish just to pander to that community. Even our immigration policy treats them differently then it does all other immigrants coming to our country. If they set foot on American soil they get to stay. That policy does not extend itself to any other illegal immigrants. They got paramilitary groups training in the Everglades toward the day when the United States will declare war on Cuba."

"Why they ever let that clown get in there in the first place? Why didn't the people fight to keep him out? Hey, freedom comes with a price—sometimes you have to die and sacrifice for others."

Ivan sighed a long sigh.

"Vinnie, I'm just telling you what the deal is. They're tired of waiting and they see a powerful crime boss who wants to settle in Florida as the perfect answer to their prayers. Salsa says they have a plan already. It will only take two men. They fly over in your airplane, land on the North side of the Island, and his contacts will give them the plan when they get there. What do you want me to tell him? It's all up to you."

I ran my hands over my eyes. "Okay, tell Pete and Santo to get ready for a special job. Tell them they're going to use the plane that will make them happy as pigs in shit. Now, we got any more business cause I want to go home."

"Just a few things more." Ivan seemed hesitant to tell me what they were.

'What, what, already?"

"Don't be so edgy, Vin, I just want to talk to you about the sale of your properties."

That kind of perked me up.

"Well, did we sell the Diamond Wheel?"

"Yes, yes, to the city service agency. We made a very nice profit."

"I tell you Ivan I feel like an era is ending. I loved that club from the first time I saw it."

Ivan smiled. "But, Vinnie, it was a bar, restaurant and strip joint in midtown. A dime a dozen."

I nudged him with my elbow.

"Yeah, but I did some of my best work there. Oh, by the way, remind me I have to go say goodbye to Lacy. This ain't going to be no picnic you know."

There was pain in Ivan's eyes. "Yes, I know. You were very lucky, Vinnie. But then you've always been lucky. If Rose ever found out that you had a mistress and she was pregnant—well, I think it would destroy her."

I looked into Ivan's face and understood. He was in love with Rose himself. He had wanted her from the day she first went to work for his mother.

The Friggin' Altos
A Crime Family Gone Crazy

But, as I said, he was a shy one. I often wondered what would have happened if he had asked Rose out before I did. I always wondered if she would have said yes.

"You let me worry about Rose. Now, what else." I couldn't stand the way he made me feel, like I was covered with mud and all slimy. Sometimes a man wants to be an animal in bed with a woman. Is that so bad? You don't use your wife for kinky sex. At least I don't. I liked Lacy from the first time she bumped her ass in my face. She was on the bar doing a hootchy-kootchy, and I was looking up with my mouth wide open. She was a looker all right. Not beautiful like Rose, but hot and sassy and double-jointed. How she ever allowed herself to get pregnant, I'll never know. In my mind it's up to the woman to be careful. Rubbers, salves, spermicides are for the ladies to worry about. The man's job is to perform with nothing to dull his enjoyment. If you want to be politically correct get yourself fixed. If not, take the consequences when they come.

You could have knocked me over with a feather when sassy lacy told me she was sproutin'. I was fit to be tied. I wanted to smash her face in, but I ended up making love to her and making all kinds of promises I had no intention of keeping.

LaVerne and Sam Zocco

The one promise I did intend to keep was give her money for an abortion, her telling me she was only two months pregnant, and enough money in the bank to live out her life in luxury. It was going to be a hard sell but there was no way I was going to chance a little illicit Vinnie running around. Rose might get wind of it. Sometimes news travels fast from midtown to the Island.

As for Lacy, we had our laughs, now it was time to say adios. I have to tell you she was kind of a prize for me because she was Jimmy Pecan's girl before I came into the picture. Jimmy the psycho and I had fallen out long before Lacy.

I told you he was the one that pumped the bullet into me one lonely night, over a dame no less. Anyway he could never stand being cut out of the action. He took it real hard. My shrink would say it was an ego thing with him, along with his being a control freak. We were doing all right with the gang when all this happened. We were making good profits and sharing right down the line when he gets it into his head he should be the boss.

He was a sneaky rat trying to get my gang members to turn against me. God bless Ricco and Sammy Six Toes, not to mention Pete and Santo (Frankie wasn't with me yet) and the other guys that rounded out the Friggin' Altos. They iced him right out. When he didn't kill me like he intended, he went over to Queens and started his own organization. That's one thing you could always say about Jimmy he was smart in a way only a psycho can be smart. He was ruthless and brutal and scared the piss out of everyone.

It seems incredible if you could only see what he looks like. He's tall, good looking as hell, suave, elegant, a reader who loves classical music. But he was a psycho bastard, and that's the worst kind of psycho who knows things, has the smarts of a college professor, and loves evil.

Ivan saw me remembering in my head and got off the subject of Lacy fast. What he had to tell me was worse and he knew it.

"Look, Vinnie, we sold the Cheese Factory to two guys who want to turn it into an art gallery and wine shop."

"Well that's good isn't it? What do you want me to be, orgasmic about the deal?"

Ivan flinched. "No, but there's a problem."

Oh, God, my head started to pound. "What problem?"

"When Pete and Santo whacked Tony Sweets they weren't too fussy about where they buried him." He almost ducked waiting for the explosion.

"Let me take a wild guess, here, they put him under the Cheese Factory Floor, am I right?"

"Bingo. Ricco and Sammy Six Toes dug him up early this morning, or what's left of him, and they got him on ice. They want to know what you want done with him?"

I raised my hands to heaven and asked God for an answer.

"What am I doing wrong here that you have sent me these two bunglers for cousins?" I knew he wasn't going to give me any help.

"Okay, okay, let me think. No, I know what to do right now. Tell Ricco and Sammy to dress him up like a homeless bum and take him down to the homeless shelter that used to be The Diamond Wheel. Tell them to put him in one of the cots and just leave him there. Problem solved."

Ivan looked unsure.

"Well Mr. smarty-pants Lawyer, you got a better idea? By the time they find him, we'll all be in Florida. It will take them months to identify him. It's the perfect answer."

"No, it isn't Vinnie. Don't you know they got DNA now, they will be able to identify him from his body DNA in a few days."

I couldn't believe it. "You mean to tell me this DNA stuff is one hundred percent accurate."

The Friggin' Altos
A Crime Family Gone Crazy

"Yeah, except in Los Angeles."

I wasn't even going to go there.

"Do what I tell you. Now how about The Alto Mansion. You get a realtor to sell that?"

Ivan was back to smiling. "Yes, I hired one this morning. He's right outside you want to meet him?"

"Yeah, yeah, bring him in."

I'm sitting drumming my fingers on the table when in walks Ivan with a flaming queen.

"Vinnie, this is Dana the gay realtor."

"Oh, Mister Alto, I'm just so delighted to meet you."

I look at him intensely.

"Does that patch on your jacket say, H.O.M.O."

He laughed a high pitched laugh.

"It stands for Home Ownership Means Opportunity. Isn't it just scrumptious? I want to thank you for this opportunity to serve you."

"Now listen, Dana, this is my family home you're selling. I don't want no bums living where I was born. Got it? I want respectable people living here. Is that clear?"

"Of course Mr. Alto. You just leave it to me."

And I did.

CHAPTER FIVE

Okay. So Ricco and Sammy Six Toes dig up Tony Sweet's skeleton, dress it up like a feakin' homeless bum and bring him down to the homeless shelter that was formerly The Diamond Wheel Club. They sneak past the counselor on duty, and dump him in the last cot on the left-hand side. When they reported back that all had gone well, I stopped thinking about Tony Sweets.

At the same time Frankie informed me that Carmella had asked him to drive her and Johnny Mizner to the prom. Now I had to treat this little son-of-a-bitch of a scumbag, Johnny, real good because his father was my banker. Frankie looked like he was suffering so much I was thinking of taking pity on him and telling Carmella no. But, the fact is I was so paranoid about Johnny Mizner putting hands on my pure baby, I knew Frankie had to be the one to drive them so he could keep an eye on the punk.

When I told him, Frankie looked miserable, but when I told him why he had to do it, he just gave me a wistful smile and said, okay.

At this time, only Rose and I knew that someone, some dangerous somebody had started

The Friggin' Altos
A Crime Family Gone Crazy

sending me knives and threatening notes through the mail. Every morning, when the postman arrived, there would be another evil looking dagger wrapped in a note telling me I was going to get mine soon. Rose was half out of her mind about the safety of the children, and me, I had so many enemies I couldn't begin to come up with a name of someone who really had the balls to kill me. Of course, it occurred to me that there was always Jimmy Pecan, but he was too goal oriented to be so subtle. Besides, these notes had a peculiarity about them. The writer dotted the "i" with little hearts. That little quirk seemed to take the sinister look out of the whole thing.

When I got the third dagger in a row, I called the boys together and ask them to think of anybody they had killed with a knife. I asked them to sound out the names because maybe hearing the names would jog my memory.

This was the list they could remember:

Jimmy, "The Barber," Gambini
Stuts Carmine
Nero D'Augustino
Joe Fingers
Donny "The Scum," Donato
Creepy Lazarus

Rudy Santozzi

Beans Johnson

An Evangelical Preacher (He couldn't remember which one.)

Mayor Siminelli, Mayor of one of the small towns around

Prospect Park was all he could remember.

A stockbroker, but he couldn't remember which one

Ed "The Pick," Anderson

Solly Montgomery

"Enough, enough," I howled. "I've got a headache and this ain't helping at all."

Meanwhile, Rose had a caller at the house. It was Ivan Trotsky. He finally got the nerve to visit when I wasn't there. How I know all this, you have to trust me you will find out, but just for now let me stick it in the story where it belongs.

Trotsky comes ringing the bell knowing full well I ain't there. Rose answers the door, and she herself is amazed.

"Ivan. Vinnie's not home right now."

Ivan plays it cool.

"I'm not here to see Vinnie. I wanted to talk to you about the move to Florida, and if there are any details you want me to tell you."

The Friggin' Altos
A Crime Family Gone Crazy

Rose runs her long elegant fingers through her hair and takes him by the arm, the closeness just about shattering Ivan's confidence.

"Come on down to the kitchen. We'll have coffee and talk."

That's what they did, the two of them sitting there, so close but so far.

Finally, Ivan couldn't control himself, the little weasel.

"Rose, I have loved you since the first moment you came to work for my mother. I was so shy then. I tried and tried to get up the courage to ask you out, but I just couldn't do it. You were so beautiful and I didn't know how you felt about Jewish boys. And then before I could make the big move, you up and marry Vinnie Alto. I want you to tell me if I'm wrong. I had the feeling all along that you knew how I felt about you. Is that true?"

Rose set her cup of coffee down and looked into Ivan's earnest face.

"Yes, you're not wrong. I did know. But I thought your family was so above mine that any relationship between us could never be serious. After all, your family wanted you to marry a nice Jewish girl and give them Jewish grandchildren. Any other kind of relationship would have been out of the question. I was just a little gentile girl, a Roman Catholic to boot, who scrubbed their floors and cooked."

Ivan drew his chair closer and came all the way around the table to sit by Rose. He took her hand gently.

"But if I had been more aggressive? If I had showed you how deeply I loved you and wanted you? If I could have said all those things to you to prove I was serious about you, what would your answer have been if I had asked you out?"

Those lovely blue eyes looked innocently into his black inky eyes.

"I would have said yes," Rose whispered.

That was the day Ivan began to hope. And that was the day that a little chink in Rose's loyalty to me opened up. But Rose soon realized what she had just said.

"But, of course Ivan, that's a long time in the past. I don't want to live my life thinking of things that could have been different. I made my choices in life just as you did, and now we must talk about moving to Florida and nothing else."

Poor long suffering Ivan picked up her hand and kissed it tenderly.

"Yes, Rose." He said it simply.

The Friggin' Altos
A Crime Family Gone Crazy

A long way to the North I was sitting trying to figure who could be sending me daggers and notes with hearts drawn over the letter "i." I don't know why Tony Sweets jumped into my head. I had tried to push the last time I had seen him, when I confronted him, out of my head. But, now here it was fresh and just as choking a feeling in my throat.

I remember the first thing I told him when I came into the cellar and sat down across from him was, "nice shoes, Tony."

It was then he let loose.

"Forgive me, Vinnie, forgive me! They had me dead to rights for offing that dead beat Angelo. It was going to be life, Vinnie. The books were a small price to pay for my freedom. They double-crossed me and got the search warrant early."

I took pity on the bastard.

"No harm done. Ivan Trotsky found loopholes that gave us time to switch the books. What I want to know is how could you rat me out to save your own skin? Trotsky would have saved your friggin' neck. Didn't I always take care of you—even when we were kids?"

He was blubbering and so terrified by now he was peeing himself.

"It's true, Vinnie. But, I notice lately you've changed. I thought you were losing it, Vinnie. I was afraid. Ain't you never been afraid?"

Could I stand there and tell him the truth that I was looking death in the face every second and I was even praying to God to let me off the hook. Under any other circumstances, I would have told my old friend the truth. But, I couldn't ever look weak in front of my gang. So I lied.

"Hey, Tony. The world changes, the problems get harder, life goes faster, the answers get more complicated, but Vinnie Alto never gets scared. Ricco and Six Toes will take you home. Don't let me see you around here or the Cheese Factory anymore."

When they untied him he dropped down on his knees and kissed my ring. The sweat was pouring off him, but he was so relieved he lay down on the floor and cried like a baby.

On the night he was whacked Frankie and I were playing cards at the White Palace for an alibi.

Santo and Pete never told me how they whacked him but it would have been quick, like a chop to the neck commando style. But the fact that they picked him up and drove him around for an hour before they killed him made him die a thousand times with anticipation. The moment

The Friggin' Altos
A Crime Family Gone Crazy

they stepped in front of him in the street and muscled him into the car the truth would have dawned that loyalty far outweighed childhood friendships and his old pal Vinnie was taking care of business. They did tell me he never said a word or even begged for his life. I guess he really didn't want to live in a world any longer that had lost all its civility and mercy. I think the tears he shed to himself were more for me than him.

It was the night of the prom and we were taking pictures of Carmella in her short, short gown and Johnny Mizner in his sharp tuxedo. Frankie's eyes, I noticed, were busy everywhere but looking at the happy couple.

Ivan and I had just got the call that Pete and Santo had taken off in my airplane for Cuba. In six hours they should be there and kill Castro within hours of their arrival.

The plot was simple enough. Pete would dress like an old woman in the streets of Havana and look on while Castro gave one of his long, boring speeches to keep the peoples' minds off their hunger and neediness. After the speech Castro's cavalcade of cars would wind its way past a tall building in a certain pre-ordained route. Santo would be in the window with a rifle, while Pete would be on a grassy knoll up in front of where the cavalcade had to pass. Santo would shoot from the book depository as the car passed, and Pete would shoot from the grassy knoll. It worked on JFK; it would work on Castro.

While we were waiting anxiously for word from Havana, Frankie was busy driving Carmella and Johnny to the prom. The two of them were in the back seat.

"Oh, Johnny. Yes, yes, yes." This was Carmella trying to get a rise out of Frankie by messing around with Mizner.

Johnny said something like you feel so good. Can I rub over here?

And that little wildcat Carmella said, "Yes, yes."

Frankie in the front seat couldn't help himself. He said, "Oh, God." He was crazy with lust and jealousy.

Johnny did the wrong thing then. He tapped Frankie on the shoulder and told him, "hey, Frankie, keep your eyes on the road cause real action is happening back here."

That was all she wrote.

Frankie came to a screetching halt. He jumps out of the car, opens the back seat door, and grabs this little asshole out of the back seat.

The Friggin' Altos
A Crime Family Gone Crazy

"Okay, punk, get out. You heard me. You going on your own steam or you want me to help you?"

The kid was crying for God's sake.

"I'm going, I'm going. My father's going to hear about this."

Frankie pulls out his gun. What a son-of-a-gun he is.

"Now blow." The kid goes off sniffling.

"Carmella, you come up in the front seat."

So what does Carmella do, she hustles up into the front seat. And what does she say?

"Godfather, I just love your face."

Come on, even I know what Frankie is going to say next.

"Oh, hell, slide over here and kiss me."

But, I want to tell you something about Frankie. That's all he does is just kiss her. He's got a mountain of an erection, but he's still thinking of me. What a guy. Of course the image might have just passed through his mind what the Friggin' Altos do to traitors. When I'm talking traitors I ain't talking rats like Tony Sweets. When we're talking traitors we're talking betraying the boss with his daughter. There's a special punishment for that.

LaVerne and Sam Zocco

I'm sitting in the front room when the news comes in from Havana. Not only did Pete and Santo not kill Castro, but someone had cut the gas lines to the airplane with a dagger that matches the ones I've been getting in the mail. They go down in the Florida Straits and a Cuban escaping the island in a raft and heading for Miami picked them up. Then they all got picked up by the Cuban Exile Communities organization called, "Brothers to the Rescue," and they were all brought into the United States and turned over to immigration.

Pete was still dressed as an old Cuban Lady so they released him to her cousin Vinnie, and she vouched for Santo who was dressed as a Cuban peasant, and he too was released into my custody, along with the rafter who had nobody in the United States. Out of that mess I got one great bodyguard, Emilio Gonzalez, who married our cook Dolly.

At the same time, my wife Rose gives me a note from my mother, Frances, giving me instructions where to deliver her things in Miami Beach. I gave it to Ricco to take care of, and it was then that he said, "hey that's cute." And I asked him what was cute, and he said the way my mother dotted her "i" with hearts. It was then I finally realized it was my mother who had not only been sending me knives and threatening notes

The Friggin' Altos
A Crime Family Gone Crazy

through the mail but had cut the gas lines to the plane that was carrying Pete and Santo to Havana to kill Castro. She could have killed them; she could have killed any of us.

That night I went to see her.

She was sleeping on the couch drunk as a skunk. I came in and opened some windows to let some fresh air in to kill the booze smell.

Now, my mother doesn't scare easily. I was her only child and she had brought me up right. Church every Sunday, meals on time, clean clothes and a clean house. It was wonderful to see my father and her together. He was a truck driver but he was handsome, knowledgeable, and playful. He would rub her butt when he walked by her, and they kissed when they thought I wasn't looking. He was strict but fair, my Mother only had to look at me to let me know to get busy or take the consequences that awaited disobedience. You think it was a whipping, or staying in my room, with which she punished me? Oh, no, it was going next door to Mrs. Carnetti and sitting with the old lonely widow for no less than two hours. And what did we do in those two hours? She made me sit and eat fresh-baked pizza while she reminisced to me about Sicily. She read me the agenda for the coming week from the Church's bulletin board.

She got every secret out of me concerning my love life and my hoodlum ways. Then she made me kneel with her and beg God to forgive me for another week. It was misery for a kid that wanted to be out running with his friends, but it also taught me that old people have a lot of good stuff inside, and that you'll listen to them when you won't listen to your parents. Mrs. Carnetti was my surrogate grandmother, and I learned to love her dearly.

Then the good times ended with the death of my father. He lived to be forty-seven when lung cancer stole him away right when I needed him the most. I guess I was angry at everything and everyone in my life. But most of all my anger centered on my mother. I blamed her for letting him smoke all those years. I wondered why it had to be him. If it had to be one of them, why couldn't it be my mother who would be revered as a saintly woman, and be remembered with loving thoughts? Why take my father and leave me with a mother who was a different sex from me, who didn't understand the man's world, who couldn't help me make the transition from boy to man and teach me all I needed to know about manly things? So, we looked at each other over my dad's casket

The Friggin' Altos
A Crime Family Gone Crazy

and we saw strangers looking back. She bottled up her feelings as I did, and she started to drink.

The older she got, the worse it got. She was always being brought home by the police for some minor infraction, or we had to go bail her out for the big stuff. She just didn't care anymore. It never dawned on me that she lost the love of her life, and all this attention getting behavior was to let me know she was still there. That she was a human being who you couldn't put into a chair and tell her to stay there and be quiet and not disturb the environment.

Her transgressions got weirder and weirder, and now I was dealing with a woman who seemed to be going out of her mind at last.

"Ma, you're losing it. You plow though Bloomingdales, you cut the gas lines on my plane, you send me knives and threatening notes in the mail. For God sake Ma, what are you trying to tell me?"

She lifts those blood shot eyes, her gray mop of hair, that stern face that was pretty and appealing, and stands up to her full height of five feet two inches.

"I want you to tell me what you and Mrs. Carnetti used to talk about for those two hours when you used to be sent over there? I want to be your new Mrs. Carnetti and you come and spend two hours with me a week."

For the first time since my father died, I hugged her hard against me, told her I loved her, told her how much I missed dad, and told her I'd come every week to spend time with her if she'd cut down on the booze.

That night we got drunk together.

CHAPTER SIX

I don't know if you've ever had to tell your pregnant girlfriend that you were leaving her but it's one of those situations that can get out of hand real quick.

One thing I was very smart about was never leaving a paper trail of love letters that could come back and haunt me. I wasn't too smart about leaving my girlfriend pregnant. Lacy was a good sport normally. If it were any other problem than this one she would have given me a last roll in the hay, taken the bankbook gratefully, and wished me a happy life as I tooled out the door.

Unfortunately, there are things about an easy woman that don't quite make sense. For one thing they ain't so easy. They'll do the most intimate things with you in bed, never giving a thought to whether it's moral or not to boff a married man, then in a blink of an eye they get all self-righteous when you ask them for a small favor like an abortion. Lacy may be loose, but she is very unpredictable.

I could have raised some questions of my own, you know? Like had she ever slept with Jimmy Pecan while we were together, Or, for that matter, any guy that came and went in the club. I wouldn't do that though because I didn't want her getting more hysterical than she already was. The minute she opened the door I could see I was in for a very hairy time so I switched into my tender-loving-care mode, which she wasn't buying no how.

I noticed she was putting on quite a bit of weight for someone two months pregnant. It made me wonder how big she would be if she went to full term.

She looked kinda cute, like a little girl, with her red curls bouncing around her face, her beautiful green eyes, and her baby doll pajama outfit. I suddenly realized I was slipping into my horny mode which was the worst thing I could allow myself to do at a time like this.

I took off my overcoat, brushed the snow from it, and laid it across a chair. I sat down on a rich brocade sofa. I thought it was a shame that I was forced to give all this up. It was a very nice apartment, big and airy. I wondered what Dana, the gay realtor, could get for the place if I put it on the market. Plenty, I thought. I figured Lacy might not want to hold onto the place, bad memories you know. Then I thought the last thing I should do was ever let Lacy know the place could

The Friggin' Alto's
A Crime Family Gone Crazy

be sold out from under her. I never was any good at hiding what I was thinking. Whatever popped into my mind always showed in my face. Lacy picked up on it right away; she knew what I was thinking.

She spoke to me in Brooklynese that made her voice loud, harsh and whiny.

"You're a real piece of work, Vinnie Alto. You're leaving me knocked up and used up—running out like a friggin' skunk."

I tried to move close to her. She pushed me away, her anger twisting her face up in hatred.

"Now, Lacy, settle down. Settle down. Don't go off the deep end. See I told you I'd take care of you. Here's the bankbook. There's enough money in here for the abortion, and what's left you can live on like a queen for the rest of your life."

She slapped it out of my hand and it went sailing across the room. I thought that was very rude of her.

"I don't need your friggin' money. I ain't getting no abortion.

"And don't tell me to settle down and stay calm, you can't use that stuff on me anymore. I'm a good Catholic girl. Father Gandolfo, my priest, says we need more Catholic babies. And I ain't two months pregnant; I'm six months pregnant!

And if you had any brains or thought about anyone but yourself you would have seen it for yourself."

To say I was floored was putting it mildly. Six months pregnant and she never let on for a minute. That made me very unhappy. Not only that, but who was this Father Gandolfo that was filling Lacy's head with all this shit? That made me even madder. If there's one thing I hate it's a nosy priest, especially a nosy Catholic priest.

"You tell your Father Gandolfo to have the babies. I don't want no bastard kid running around. Now you behave yourself or I'll have Ricco come over and put some sense in your head."

I was seeing red and I was getting hotter. My special feelings for Lacy were getting less and less every time she opened her big mouth. Now I ask you. You be the judge. Wasn't I doing the honorable thing by leaving her well fixed? How could I do more? than that with Rose sitting at home trusting her little heart out in me, and Carmella and Little Vinnie, what would they say if they found out their father was irresponsible? This was all Lacy's fault and I told her so in no uncertain terms.

"This is all your fault, you little bimbo. Why am I even talking to you? Why am I even offering

The Friggin' Altos
A Crime Family Gone Crazy

you this large amount of money? The kid probably ain't mine to begin with. You were batting a hundred with Jimmy Pecan before I met you, and who knows how many other guys hit the ball out of the park. Now, listen to me, honey. You can rant and rave all you want. You can still get an abortion. Tell them your health is in danger. I can get a doctor to sign a certificate in a minute that says that. I'm telling you do as I say or you ain't going to be around to spill your guts."

She laughed at me. Can you imagine this whore had the nerve to laugh at me?

"I ain't scared of you Vinnie. And you can have this friggin' apartment back too. Father Gandolfo says he has a place for me to stay until the baby's born and he'll protect me. And don't forget Jimmy Pecan is in love with me. He ain't going to take kindly to you saying mean things about me sleeping around. So take your blood money and get out of here."

I could see the blood in her eyes. In that state a woman is liable to do anything to express her hostility. I turned compassionate again.

"Lacy, baby, Jimmy Pecan is a psycho. He's my worst enemy. We hate each other's guts. Now do what I tell you and stop fighting me. I know your in a tight spot, but there's a very simple answer, get rid of the kid. It will make everybody happy. I know you're just doing this because you're unhappy I'm dumping you, but believe me, I got to move to Florida. The plans are made; there's no backing out. It's killing me inside to leave you like this after all you've meant to me. You don't want to break up my family, Lacy. My wife would be devastated; my kids would hate me. If you love me you won't do this to me. Now do what I tell you and stay away from that nut Pecan."

I thought it was a pretty good speech. It seemed to calm her but, of course, I had misread her. For the first time I saw what a vindictive woman she really was.

"If you think Jimmy is such a psycho, you better tell Little Vinnie that because he hangs around him all the time. And here's a news flash for you, Jimmy Pecan is moving to Florida too. The apartment is all yours. Now get out of here you friggin' Alto."

I could see it was the best deal I was going to get.

When I got back home there was more trouble waiting. The moment the door closed Ricco was on top of me.

"We got trouble boss."

It made me laugh.

The Friggin' Altos
A Crime Family Gone Crazy

"Tell me something else that's new."

He looked at me laughing and scratched his head.

"Boss, this is serious. The boys did what you said to do with Tony Sweets. They dressed him up like a homeless bum and left him in the homeless shelter on a cot. But the counselor, at the shelter, spotted him right away. He called the cops."

I just couldn't get all worked up over Sweets after Lacy.

"So what. So they found a skeleton. It'll take them some time to identify him. We're leaving for Florida in a couple of days. We're home free."

"Except for one little thing, boss."

"What, what."

"He was still wearing those snakeskin shoes. The cop who came out recognized them right away. They want you to come in for questioning."

Meanwhile, upstairs, Frankie was in Carmella's room trying to deal with my seventeen-year-old daughter. I think I forgot to tell you that Johnny Mizner's father, my banker, called me and told me what Frankie had done to his scumbag son. I had confronted Frankie immediately. His song and dance was that the boy was being fresh with Carmella in the back seat of the car on the way to the prom, and he couldn't stand this kid pawing

Carmella. It made him see red, he said. So he threw the kid out of the car and told him to blow. Was I suspicious, did I think Frankie had the hots for Carmella? No. I thought he was being a wonderful godfather to his goddaughter. So I gave him orders to go get a hold of that fucken kid and break a few of his fingers for touching Carmella. We both laughed when I said he should never be able to play the piano again.

Frankie was suffering. I know that now. Like I said he was in Carmella's room upstairs in the mansion.

"I must be friggin' crazy. I go and break a kid's fingers for touching you and I can't stop myself from wanting to do the same thing. You drive me wild, baby."

Carmella is loving it.

"I told you I'll never tell Daddy. I love you so much, Frankie. You got to let me have all of you or I'll kill myself."

What could Frankie do? He let himself be sucked in by this temptress. He should have known better. He knew the Sicilian code very well. You touch the boss's daughter, you pay big time.

Did he love me or my daughter? He should have loved me more.

I have to give him credit though. He wasn't giving in easy.

"All right, Carmella, all right already. I'll find some place where we can be alone. But it'll have to wait until we get settled in Florida."

At that precise minute I remember standing at the bottom of the stairs and calling up to Frankie.

"Hey Frankie, you upstairs?"

His response came back immediately.

"I'm in the guestroom playing solitaire on the computer."

"Well get down here, you got to drive me down to the police station."

Carmella told me long afterward what was in her mind when Frankie walked out the door.

"Frankie, take the express. This bod won't wait—get it while it's hot, Frankie. Please, get it while it's hot."

You got to love a seventeen-year-old and how they express themselves these days.

So Frankie drove me down to the police station. I wasn't a bit worried. We owned every cop in the joint. It was Detective Abdullah who gave me the shocking news about Tony Sweets.

"Detective Abdullah. I'm very saddened to hear you have found my ex-partner Tony Sweets in this condition. All I can tell you is I haven't seen

LaVerne and Sam Zocco

him for over a month. He just ups and took off. Now, we find he is dead. Ain't life a bitch? I think his mother would be grateful if you would release his skeleton to the Morning Side Funeral Home and we will give him the funeral he deserves. I hope you find the rat that did this."

Abdullah was an all right guy. He had only been on my payroll for a few months, but he knew all the right things to say. However, he was also warning me that the police were going to come down hard on me moving to Florida, and maybe make trouble, unless I helped them identify the killer of Tony Sweets. They knew very well I knew who killed him.

"Mr. Alto, we were hoping you could help us." Abdullah spoke in a very New Delhi Indian accent. "Here are the snakeskin shoes Tony was wearing when we found him. If you would just give the shoes to the person you think killed him, and call us to tell us who you gave them to, we will pick him up for Tony's murder. In return, we will make no fuss when you are off to sunny Florida. As for the arrangements to release the bones of Tony Sweets immediately to his mother, consider it done."

It was easy enough. I just give the shoes to some schmuck and call Abdullah and tell him who

I gave the shoes to. I could give them to a stranger and call, and the police would grab the poor guy within minutes. They wouldn't have any evidence to convict him, but they could keep him on the hot seat answering questions for days. By that time The Friggin' Altos would be long gone. It was a win, win situation for all of us.

On our way out of the police station I told Frankie to send Det. Abdullah a thousand dollars for his help. I also told him to send another thousand to the Pakistani Defense Fund. I like to cover all my bases.

When I arrived home, tired and worn out from the day, and under a great deal of stress, who should greet me but Dana, the gay realtor, with what he thought was wonderful news.

"Well, we are just so happy, Mr. Alto. You'll never guess. We sold the house. I'm sure it is going to please you no end, and you will be very happy with the new owners."

Now this was more like it.

"Hey, that's great and fast. I hope you remembered that I am very sentimental about this house. I was born here, all the Altos were born here. Okay, go ahead and tell me, who are the new owners?"

"The Catholic Church just bought it. Their representative, Father Gandolfo, was just here with the money. He is opening a home for unwed pregnant women. He said he already has his first case, a poor unfortunate named Lacy Love."

Then Rose chimes in.

"Oh Vinnie. You are so wonderful. Just think, down the line, Miss Lacy Love's child can say Vinnie Alto is responsible for me being here."

Dana was all hip-hop with joy.

"Ill bet you feel like giving me something nice for making you so proud."

"Yeah, I'd like to give you something."

We both seemed to have the same idea at the same time.

"Well, Mr. Alto, how about those really lovely snakeskin shoes your holding?"

"You want them—they're all yours."

Then I went straight to the phone and called Det. Abdullah and told him who would be wearing the shoes so they could pick him up.

Just another day in Paradise.

CHAPTER SEVEN

And so we moved to Florida. And so life got interesting again. Our Global Company was taking a hefty chunk out of the country's economy and that was good news. You may wonder, then, what did I care about the chump change I could squeeze out of the three Miami crime bosses? I told you my gang and our operation were separate from our world enterprises and gave me the chance to play boss with full control and power. I told you criminals never think like you justice-lovers. Criminals want more, more and more. They're always thinking up new and dangerous ways of adding to the pot. Let the brain trusts like Trotsky dream of cornering the world's money market, I was happy with my smaller desires to own the three crime bosses' actions in Miami. Doing crimes is like the game, "Monopoly". You pit your cunning and muscle against the other guy's to see who wins Boardwalk and Park Place. It's the win that's everything. Listen, if we criminals were allowed to use our sliminess in legitimate operations, we'd have owned the world a long time ago. As it is, we only own half.

LaVerne and Sam Zocco

If it were all about money I would have retired when I was twenty-five. But it ain't all about money. It's about being slippery, planning your moves way in advance, and pouncing when the time is right. Tragically, it is also about murdering your opponent when they don't want to say "uncle." All us criminals are very hard headed. We never want to believe there isn't some underhanded trick we can use to beat the system. That's why so many of us go to jail, we won't call it quits until the cell door slams, and then not even then. It's about being in on the action, that challenge that keeps me going. I don't want to be King of the World; I just want the name Vinnie Alto to stand for a man who was unbeatable.

There was something inside me I carried around since I was a little kid. It was an intense admiration for the greatest Crime Boss who ever lived, Al Capone. For you younger crowd out there, Al was an Italian kid who ruled Chicago, and rose to be the biggest gangster of the Nineteen Twenties and Thirties.

He dressed elegantly for a big slob, played opera music while he was killing his enemies with a baseball bat, smoked big Havana cigars, and had a long scar that ran the length of his cheek.

The Friggin' Altos
A Crime Family Gone Crazy

If you tried to come up with such a character for a book you would discard him as too flamboyant, too evil, too outrageous, and too unbelievable. That's exactly what made Al great. He had a "catch me if you can," attitude about the cops, he sneered openly at the City officials, who by the way, were all on his payroll, and he gave newspaper interviews portraying himself as an innocent and beloved man who was just making a living. He also denigrated FBI agent, Eliot Ness, who the Director of the Agency, J. Edgar Hoover, had sent to end Capone's "Reign of Terror." If only Capone had known that J. Edgar was, shall we say, more flamboyant than Al, he would have ended that guy's life with a real Sicilian send-off.

This is the man who ordered the "St. Valentine Day Massacre," that killed seven lowly minions of an opposing crime boss. It was done in broad daylight, with innocent people walking the streets. What a guy! It was spraying machineguns everywhere, and afterward he had the balls to tell the reporters he was not such an uncivilized monster to do such a thing without regard for innocent bystanders.

He was the undisputed King of a vast empire, so vast that between him and his enforcers were a hundred layers of underlings transmitting his orders and isolating him from being arrested. He was always someplace else at the time of the mayhem. It was a full proof scheme. He could have gone on forever, but he made one stupid mistake. Hey, I'm not being disrespectful when I say that. Even he would admit he was an idiot. He forgot to pay Uncle Sam his fair share of taxes on all his illegal profits. The government didn't give a flying fuck if they were illegal or legal. If he had come across with the dough, and not been so greedy, they wouldn't have slammed the tax codebook on his head so hard. When he woke up he was listening to Caruso, the Pavarotti of his day, in a jail cell where he died of all things, syphilis. What a fucking hero he was to me. Like an Italian Robin Hood, only taking from the poor and giving the loot to himself.

Anyway, in researching where I wanted to live in Florida, I was hot for Al Capone's Mansion out on Palm Island right off the Venetian Causeway. Trotsky checked into it for me, but to my disappointment it was privately owned and not for sale at any price. I could have made them sell, but why start a big brouhaha on my first day in the State. So I settled for the Mansion next door that was down on the point of the island. I snapped it

The Friggin' Altos
A Crime Family Gone Crazy

up for the New Alto Mansion and headquarters for my business.

I was like a kid as we settled into the new house over the next few months. It was like heaven to get out of those Armani suits and into shorts and tank tops. It took me a while to get used to wearing flip-flop sandals but I adjusted.

One of my favorite things was taking long walks around the estate, sitting on the sea wall and watching the giant, gentle Manatees coming and going. There were palm trees everywhere, mountains of fallen coconuts on the ground, and such a breeze you wouldn't believe. It blew my hair down over my tanned face and made my "St. Jude," holy medal swing in the wind. I'd been wearing that medal since I found out my bullet was on the move.

Happy as I was, the old feeling of being out of the action made me antsy. Finally, I told Trotsky to contact the three crime bosses for a meeting. I didn't know at the time, but the three crime bosses had already had a meeting about me.

This was the agreement they came to amongst themselves. Because I was a known quantity to them having done their research about my history and reputation, they felt staging an all out war would be futile. They also had looked up Jimmy

Pecan and came to this conclusion. It didn't take a rocket scientist for them to see that Pecan was the most terrifying threat of the two of us, and because he was psycho and I was a more reasonable depressive. They rightly decided if they could get me and Pecan fighting each other, it would be to their advantage. Unlike Pecan, who was insane in a bigger way than me, he would be the one to resort to any dangerous actions to get what he wanted, which was all of their businesses. In me they saw a more settled nut because I had to be more stable with a wife and kids and more restrained in my paybacks. Not that I wouldn't slit their throats if I had to, but I would do it only after sitting down and thinking about what it would mean to Rose and the Kids. Rose and the kids would have argued with that, but anyway that's how they saw it. They decided to deal me in to a good part of the action, if, I, in return, would protect them from Jimmy Pecan.

That's what they decided, but along with that, they didn't want to appear that they were just caving in to my demands, it would make them look weak. And they couldn't come out with guns drawn because they didn't want to anger me to the point where I would start a war. So they thought up a humorous way to warn me that they all came from mysterious and powerful heritages and, at the same time, politely asked me to go back home.

That's why the night after my invitations were received by all three, Overlord Pierre of the Haitians, Lazaro Salsa of the Cubans, and Chief Panther Bob of the Miccosukee Tribes, I was awakened by activity out on my lawn.

"Jeez, it's three o'clock in the morning. What the hell is that drum beating and man singing out on our lawn?"

Rose asked me sleepily. "What is it Vinnie, it sounds spooky." I got up and took a good look out the window.

"Holy Merda. It's a Voodoo priest wailing some mumbo jumbo. Where's my gun?" That's when Little Vinnie came running in.

"Hey, Pop, you see that guy, cool. He's wearing feathers, his face is painted all white, and some other guy with him looks like a zombie."

The kid really exasperated me at times.

"Stay with your mother, I'm going out to talk to him."

Rose grabbed my arm. "Be careful, Vinnie—they got powers to turn people into the living dead."

LaVerne and Sam Zocco

I thought of Mick Jaegger, Rudy Giuliani, and Pat Riley. If you don't know who they are, you got no business reading this book.

When I walked out onto the lawn I was just about messing in my pants. It wasn't so much the tall, lanky, priest; it was this fucker standing next to him. He was a real zombie with dead eyes and a lifeless face. He stood maybe seven feet tall and he had a well-edged machete in his right hand.

"Hey you—yeah you. Come here. What do you think your doing with your drum beating and your wailing this time of the morning?"

The priest raised his Voodoo pole.

"Overlord Pierre, Mon., has just put a curse on you, Mon. Mon, he say you get gone out of Florida before he send Mongo here, the Zombie, with his machete to kill your whole family. Is there an answer?"

"Oh there's an answer, alright."

That's when I put a bullet in Mongo, the Zombie's, left leg. He carried on something awful, whining like a baby. The priest backed away in sheer terror.

"Mon, oh, Mon. You shoot Mongo. Are you crazy?"

I went up to him and grabbed a handful of feathers he was wearing by his crotch.

The Friggin' Altos
A Crime Family Gone Crazy

"Take your drums, your feathers and Mongo here back to your boss. Tell him to be at my meeting. Now scram out of here before I ram your Voodoo rod down your mouth."

Half-dragging, half-bumping Mongo on some rocky patches, the priest fled into the night.

The next night I got my answer from Lazaro Salsa, the Cuban drug King and activist.

Again right around three in the morning, I hear a chicken screeching on my lawn.

"Jeez, Rose, what the hell is that? Rose, Rose, wake up. There's a guy out on the lawn killing a chicken."

Rose was wide-awake.

"I read about this. That's a Santeria High Priest from Cuba conducting a Santeria Ritual."

Once again I got my gun out.

Little Vinnie comes running in. "Pop, did you hear that?

"Yeah. Now stay here with your mother. I'm going out to talk to him."

Rose was standing up and peeking through the window.

"Be careful, Vinnie. They got powers from dead bones they dig up in cemeteries."

I let out a sneering laugh.

"If that's what it takes, I got more dead bones then he does, only they ain't laying around in cemeteries." I was thinking of all my enemies in New York who were in the Hudson, the Atlantic and just plain boneless. "Ain't no Italian who don't know about making bones." That was an obscure reference to your first kill for the mob.

This time the priest was a skinny, dark-skinned runt with a live chicken in his hands.

"Hey, Senor. What do you think you're doing?"

He got right to the point.

"Lazaro Salsa says, get out of town or he's going to wring your neck like I do this chicken. You no kill Castro. You got no power."

Well, that hurt even if it was true about Castro.

I took that fucking chicken and wrung it's neck right up in front of the guy's face. He suddenly turned white.

"Now eat it." I ordered it in the deepest, raspiest voice I could muster. My voice is raspy normally, but this was the voice they used in "The Exorcist," for the devil.

He started to cry, poor guy.

"Have mercy, Senor."

"Eat!"

The Friggin' Altos
A Crime Family Gone Crazy

There was the sound of munching on chicken bones and raw flesh.

"Now go back to your boss and tell him I expect him at the meeting. It's okay. You can spit the feathers out now."

You might think they would have given up. But, no they didn't. The next night I heard whooping on the lawn. I could see through the window a big red campfire and this warrior dancing a rain dance around it. In my mind, I thought Chief Panther Bob must have hated this terrible stereotype, but a promise made to crime bosses is a promise kept.

This time Rose didn't have to tell me it was the Miccosukee. I always thought that was a great name for a car. This warrior was dressed in nothing but a skimpy skirt dancing around the fire. He was swinging a hatchet up and down in his right hand.

Little Vinnie came running in again.

He vexed me.

"Don't you ever sleep? Take care of your mother."

When I walked up to the warrior he stopped dancing. He stood there with so much dignity I had to admire him.

"Excuse me, but you're on private property."

He had a deep voice but the accent was from the old Cowboy and Indian movies.

"Chief Panther Bob say you leave land of Fathers by next full moon or he sleep in Sauna for vision of how to kill you."

Well, right there I knew he was kidding. It used to be sweat lodge, but he had slipped and told the truth. The Chief had a sauna.

"He's tough, huh?"

"Not Chief Panther Bob, or even the council, but Princess Snow Feather, she's a bitch."

"How come they all got those Indian names in this day and age?"

He relaxed from his stony pose.

"Aw, it's just for the tourist. We got sweat lodges on Tamiami Trail, but it's more fun taking up the Lear Jet." Then he remembered what he was doing and stiffened up again.

"Hey, I like you. You're a gentleman. What's your name?"

"Miccosukee or real name?"

"Both."

"I am called Long Loincloth by the tourists, but my real name is Adam Billy."

I couldn't let him get away with no punishment so while he was talking I picked up a faggot from

The Friggin' Altos
A Crime Family Gone Crazy

the fire and burned his long loincloth leaving him buck-naked.

"Now you're Naked Buns. Tell the Chief I expect him at my meeting."

There were tears in his eyes, but he never showed a sign of pain.

"By the way, use some Aloe on those burns, it's wonderful for everything down here."

The meeting with the three crime bosses went smooth as glass after that. Overlord Pierre gave me part of the smuggling action, and the extortion business. In return, I let him keep his Port-a-Princes nightclub and gave him Ricco to watch the split.

Lazara Salsa gave me part of the drug and balleta action, and I let him keep his Mambo Club. I gave him Sammy Six Toes as my representative.

Chief Panther Bob gave me a half interest in one of his casinos, and asked that Little Vinnie be sent to his daughter Snow Feather who would run the Casino for me.

In return for all this benevolence, I was expected to deal with Jimmy Pecan and make sure he didn't try to enlarge his new organization at their expense. I told them it was a piece of cake.

I had heard Jimmy Pecan had bought a club called the New Moon over on South Beach and

LaVerne and Sam Zocco

had settled into a Mansion on Star Island, not too far from mine.

After the meeting, Rose asked me if I would take her out to see the town. Now that my business was all done, I felt like celebrating too. I told her we'd have appetizers at Laurenzo's, and stop at Macaroni's in Lauderdale. She asked me if we could go dancing and I told her like Fred and Ginger. Only I wanted to take a walk on the beach first.

I was sitting there alone listening to the seagulls and the ocean waves lapping the shore, when a mysterious thing happened.

"Hi," It was a breathless woman's voice.

"Jeez, you scared me. I'm losing my touch I never even heard you coming."

"Do you mind if I share your piece of driftwood?"

I want you to know this woman was beautiful. She looked like Marilyn Monroe in her prime, before the Kennedys and all that unpleasantness. Her perfume blew my socks off, and I crouched over to hide the start of a woody.

"Sure," I said, "park it."

She sat down real close.

"Beautiful evening."

I smiled my best smile.

The Friggin' Altos
A Crime Family Gone Crazy

"It is now."

So we started talking. I told her I was new in town, that I had just bought a house in the area. She right away starts to seduce me telling me I look like Antonio Banderas only more sexy and tanned. Well, I come back telling her she looks like Monroe only more sexy and tanned. Then all of a sudden she jumps up.

"I gotta go." That's all she says and starts running away.

"Hey," I yell at her, "you didn't even tell me your name."

From a long distance away she calls to me.

"Just call me Marilyn." And she's gone.

All night long trying to show Rose a good time, I couldn't get Marilyn out of my mind. There was something familiar about her but I just couldn't put my finger on it. When Rose started to get sore cause I wasn't paying too much attention, I let it go. But, she haunted me nevertheless.

CHAPTER EIGHT

For a few weeks nothing happened. The most exciting thing I did was buy a chunk of land right in back of the Miami City Hall out towards Biscayne Bay and next to Dodge Island.

Little Vinnie was antsy waiting for his good friend, Crayton Hooks to graduate from Harvard Law School in June. Crayton promised Little Vinnie he would come down to Florida after he got his sheepskin and vacation with his friend while he waited for answers to his job applications.

The few times I met Crayton he called me "The Vinman," and suckered me into believing, though I already knew better, he was right off the streets and living in a ghetto. Nothing could be further from the truth.

For some reason Little Vinnie liked to tape his phone calls and it was an accident that I turned the machine on one day to hear this exchange between Little Vinnie and Crayton.

"Crayton, m'man. Late with the ring-a-ding-ding. Aloha from Florida. Are you hanging As, Bs, or Cs?" Crayton comes back in this funky voice. "Funky fool. Dude getting chronic, in the posse with whoppers and poppers. Teachers, mofo—chics, potty mouthed and fab. You flying, bro?"

"I'm tooling the broads. Grab your sheepskin, hang a right at Tallahas, man. Keep your dreadlocks tight; sculpt the bod—yo to Ma and Pa. Missing your face. Let me hear how you're going to sound in court."

Crayton in a Yuppie Voice.

"Ladies and gentlemen of the jury. My client, Vinnie Alto is innocent. He is an upstanding man of the community, and would never, ever entertain thoughts of crime against the fabric of our society.

"Sailing with the voice-o-gram. Hitting the tom-tom—(spells) b-y-e, b-y-e. Later Dude."

Now admit it, ain't that a howl. Crayton lived in both worlds, black and white, and he could fool them both. Smart.

Then a strange thing started to happen to me. It was so frightening I ran to see Dr. Ruth who had taken me up on my offer. For the first time I really thought I was crazy.

I guess I looked really panicky because the doc commented on how pale I was looking right through my tan.

"What I say to you really don't go no farther. Right?"

LaVerne and Sam Zocco

"Not unless you kill someone, destroy property, abuse someone or want to commit suicide in my office." She could always make me laugh.

"Well, one out of three ain't bad." I kidded her like that. "Nah, I'm just kidding. It's nothing like that. It's something I ain't told no one up to now. Just tell me you'll keep your beautiful mouth shut, and I'll spill what's happening."

"Vinnie," she says with that sincere smile, "I've always told you, you can tell me anything. I'm not your judge—I'm here to help you deal with your stress, not preach to you."

"Okay, here goes. I've been seeing the ghost of Al Capone in my house. He comes to me late at night when I'm in the kitchen drinking wine."

She looks at me like I got two heads.

"Oh, Vinnie."

I moved to the front of the couch. "No, no, it's true. I was sitting there just thinking about my life and suddenly there he was—the cigar, the twenties clothes, big time gangster from the old days. He cooked me veal and peppers."

She wanted to show me how crazy I sounded.

"Why would he be in your kitchen?"

I had an answer for that right away. "He tells me he wants to help me run my business. He says he's got a lot of time on his hands and he misses the excitement. He says he paid off the screws—you know, down below. I feel sorry for the guy."

A look of great concern came across her face. I was wondering what her reaction would be if I told her about the bullet.

"It's a delusion, Vinnie. You're under so much stress you feel you need help so you conjured this hero of yours up. Don't you get it?"

I came right back at her.

"He said you'd say that, so he gave me this to give to you."

There was real amazement on her face as she looked at Al Capone's driver's license issued in 1932 to Alfonse Capone. "This is a joke, right? No, never mind. I have the feeling if I checked this out, it would be true.

"Okay, you're seeing the ghost of Al Capone. Do you think you could get him in for a session? I'd be real interested to hear him tell me why he is answering your cry for help. Don't you see Vinnie; this is a cry for help. You're making believe that Al is giving you advice so you don't get blamed for all the awful things you've been doing."

I had to give her that. "Maybe you're right—but he plays a helluva game of "bocce" ball. Oh, by the way, I also met a mysterious woman on the Beach named Marilyn."

I can now tell you about what was going on with Jimmy Pecan at this time cause I know the whole story. He spilt his guts when the time came and here's one of the meetings he had that was especially interesting. Here comes the kicker that I knew nothing about.

My mystery woman, Marilyn, is sitting in Jimmy's office at the Blue Moon. Surprised? They were talking about our meeting on the beach.

"Jimmy, it was a cinch. He's sitting there and I could have blown him away. He never heard me coming." Nice broad, right?

Smooth Jimmy is suspicious, the donut head.

"That don't sound like Vinnie. Where were his bodyguards?"

"He was all alone, I tell you. There was no one. I think the bum is losing it."

"Good, cause I'm going to give him a little present so he knows I mean business. I want my cut from the three crime bosses but they bought Vinnie to protect them. I want you to get a job in his strip joint when it opens. Pay him some visits after the shows, get him worked up, you know what I mean."

Now here comes the skinny on Marilyn.

"Okay, okay, but I want you to know I'm only doing this for Lacy. She was my little sister and she died in childbirth. I told her Vinnie Alto was a bum. Now she's dead, and he's got to pay. I'm going to tie that bum up for you, but I want to be there when you finish him off. I want it done now!"

"Hey, didn't I love Lacy too. I promise. The day Vinnie Alto gets shot you'll be there."

"NOW!"

"Patience. He'll get his soon."

Well, now, you see you don't know everything. I'll bet you thought this broad was on the make for me like I did. It's understandable. But there's always a joker in the deck. You learn that when you're in the organization. I even told Dr. Ruth about my suspicions.

"You met a mystery woman on the beach? This sounds romantic."

See she's as gullible as you are.

"She was a beauty all right. I can't help thinking there was something familiar about her." See I was putting two and two together trying to come up with Lacy but my memory wasn't helping me.

"She must have made a real impression on you."

LaVerne and Sam Zocco

"Yeah, she did."

"In what way?" I love it when Dr. Ruth probes for secrets.

"She got within touching distance of me and I never heard her coming. I got the feeling she knew my bodyguards weren't there."

Dr. Ruth got alarmed.

"What are you thinking?"

"It just hit me—I think I'm being stalked by a beautiful woman."

"If that's true, doesn't it worry you?"

"No, it interests me. I think I'm looking forward to the next time I meet Marilyn. I just know there will be a next time."

My new restaurant and strip club was almost finished. As soon as I got the liquor license I was gong to throw a big grand opening party and invite all the crime bosses, their people, all the respectable wealthy citizens up to Palm Beach, my gang and the City fathers.

I had named the club, "Dante's Inferno," after the Italian Poet's poem about a trip through hell. Where Jimmy Pecan's club, The New Moon, was all Art Deco with mirrors and blue lights, a big band and a great singer named Queenie Smith; the Inferno was a red and black cave that was mysterious and scary.

The Friggin' Altos
A Crime Family Gone Crazy

Both clubs had caused a lot of attention from The Miami Herald, the local newspaper, and the big bucks we had both spent on publicity and advertising already had people chomping at the bit waiting for them to open.

I was feeling pretty dirty and guilty about Rose for almost ruining her big night out thinking about Marilyn, so I arranged a special night for us at the almost completed Inferno. Frankie hired a cook and seen to the recorded music. The campagne was on ice when Rose and I came though the doors. Rose looked beautiful in a blue silk evening gown and diamonds. She even wheedled me into wearing a tux.

There were red lights that were placed strategically around the place, to light up all the walls like they were on fire. The black tables, chairs, bars, drapes, dishes and silverware were elegant. Only the centerpicccs of silver candlesticks and holders relieved the eerie feel of the place.

Rose and I were drinking wine together, telling each other how much we loved each other when I see Frankie out of the corner of my eye waving his hands around trying to get my attention.

At first I thought he was trying to be funny. But he kept it up and kept it up, until I excused myself and left Rose sitting at the table for two in front of the big windows while I went to Frankie to find out what the fuck he wanted.

"What is it, Frankie, you're acting like a jumping bean?"

"The cook in the kitchen ain't the one I hired for tonight. He's been on the phone forever. Now, I can't find him."

THEN ALL HELL BROKE LOOSE!

Suddenly, the windows shattered blowing large pieces of razor sharp glass inward spraying anything in their paths with a sparkly icicle storm so dense it clouded the air like fog. I screamed for Rose. I found myself down on my knees where Frankie had thrown me, fighting to get up to find Rose. Frankie held on to me until the Uzzi Machineguns stopped firing and an eerie calm settled over the room. Frankie had saved my life.

Through the buzzing sound of the Uzzis I heard Rose screaming for me but now the screams had stopped too. I struggled out of Frankie's hands and jumped to my feet. I was covered with glass.

Across the large expanse of restaurant I could see the area where Rose had been sitting at the table when I left her. There was a huge hole in the wall there now that framed the peaceful Bay outside only a few hundred feet away. There was no sign of Rose, only rubble, glass window splinters and brick wall debris.

I ran crying, weeping and screaming, across the room.

"Rose, Rose."

I started digging in the mound of rubble for a few minutes with my bare hands and fingernails bleeding red like the walls. I felt Frankie beside me digging too, both of us crazy with fear.

Then both of us heard the moan off to the left of the fallen wall and huge hole. We scrambled to the spot and saw a flash of diamond and a patch of blue silk under the pieces of concrete and glass.

We dug down to Rose in minutes. Thank God, she was breathing. I pulled hard to drag her into the red lights. I was by her arms and Frankie was by her feet. Her face was covered with glass splinters that had stuck in her skin. Worse, much worse, her eyes were bloodied, glass sticking in the lids, and particles under the lids directly in her eyes.

I held her, rocking her, while Frankie went for help.

She moaned and groaned but she was mercifully out of it. I wanted to pick at the splinters but I didn't dare. A couple of times she tried to lift her eyelids. The fluttering caused her to scream in pain and me to cry harder telling her to stop, stop. The pain finally made her aware it was a bad idea and she seemed to fall into a deep sleep for which I was grateful.

I spent the whole night at the hospital. Finally, the doctors told me there was a 50-50 chance my Rose would be blind. They wouldn't know for a few months when the bandages would come off. For now they had cleaned her eyelids and eyes of splinters. The rest was up to God.

You would think seeing what my actions had done to the most beloved thing in my life, I would quit the business and retire.

Instead, I was sitting in the kitchen drinking a glass of wine plotting revenge against Jimmy Pecan when Al Capone showed up.

"Vinnie."

"Oh, hi, Mr. Capone. I didn't hear you—I got a lot on my mind."

"Call me Al, Vinnie. How's Rose?" There was that slight Italian accent.

"Doctors say she has a 50-50 chance of losing her sight. They have to wait until the bandages come off to be sure of anything. Another month or so they say."

The Friggin' Altos
A Crime Family Gone Crazy

"I'm sorry Vinnie. There's no more family protection in the mob. In my day it was man to man, and done with honor."

"You mean like the St. Valentine Day Massacre?"

"You see, Vinnie, that's what I mean. It was my fatal flaw, arrogance. It made me explosive and lose my temper. I thought I should get everything I wanted. I thought I was a big man."

"Could have been the syphilis too."

"Perhaps. Anyway I played right into Eliot Ness's hands. What a bulldog he was. I'm smarter now. This insult to your family honor is personal with me and must be revenged. I want to help you."

"I been sitting here for hours trying to think of a way to get that rat, Pecan."

"You're not going to call in Brutto Demenza?"

"No, Brutto is only for the big jobs."

"Then, I think I know how to do it if you'll just listen to me."

I listened and I liked it. I went right to work putting Al's plan into action.

CHAPTER NINE

I figured while Rose was safe in the hospital, it would be a good time to take a crack at killing off Pecan. Whatever you may think of Al Capone, he had a wonderful philosophy for revenge. As we sat in my kitchen eating cannelloni pasta and drinking Chianti wine, Al told me his plan and I could see right away it was beautiful.

"Vinnie, if you want the perfect revenge on Jimmy Pecan you got to find out what he loves the most in the world. I don't mean women or money, but what really gets to his soul. Something or someone he trusts with all his secrets and that he would give his life for."

I was leery. "Al, a man like Pecan don't love anything but himself. He's got no soul."

Al spilled a little wine on his double-breasted suit. "Oh yes he does. Every man has something. Something that would near kill him if he lost it. Isn't there some little nothing that you feel that way about?"

I had to admit he was right.

"Yeah, yeah. It's a little replica of a bulldozer my Dad gave me on my tenth birthday. He was a Teamster—drove heavy equipment. I carry it around like a good luck charm. I guess I love it because it was the last thing he gave me—it's my connection to him."

Al sat back and burped in satisfaction.

"And you can bet Jimmy Pecan has something just like it. You find it, you destroy it! You need someone to go over and snoop around Pecan's house. Put bugs in the house, listen to what he does when he's alone."

"You're right. I'll get Frankie on it right away. Thanks Al. But, you know it ain't going to kill Pecan outright."

"That's true or it may not be true. We'll see what you do with the information. But, you can always kill Pecan and you will. But this is better. It may not kill Pecan outright, but it will be the death of his soul."

I sent Frankie over the next day to bug Pecan's house. He had a lot of guards around, but Frankie was slick. He'd find a way. Even with all that equipment, and do it right in front of their noses.

I was thinking and thinking about what Jimmy might love that I could whack. I called Frankie in to catch me up on some information I didn't know. When he told me I was floored.

"Frankie, I want you to find out what happened to Lacy. She is Jimmy Pecan's closest friend. She's the only one he has ever cared about."

Frankie turned pale and seemed a whole lot uncomfortable.

"Well, well, what's wrong? You're looking like you seen a ghost."

"Gee, Vin, didn't you hear? Lacy died in childbirth. I thought you knew."

If he had opened me up with a knife I couldn't have been more surprised.

"You're giving me a turn of the knife here. I can't believe it. Little Lacy. She was a great babe. A little on the vindictive side. This makes me very sad."

"Rumor is, Jimmy's already got a new love that he's keeping under wraps."

I said a "Hail Mary," for Lacy, then got right on with business.

"We gotta find out who this new broad is. Me and a friend been talking it over and we think you should bug Pecan's house and get the lowdown on what he's up to, and who he shares his life with. I want you to go over and do that. I know, I know, you don't have to tell me that it's dangerous work, a lot of guards hanging around, but you can do it. You always manage a way to charm anybody.

Ain't that right." I mussed up his hair with my hand.

"It's a piece of cake. Jimmy takes most of his crowd to The New Moon at night. He leaves maybe two at the most at the house.

"Don't worry I'll get the job done and nobody will be the wiser."

I kinda wanted him to disappear after that so I could be alone to think. But, he kept standing there, rocking back and forth on his toes. He only did that when he had something to tell me he was afraid of telling me.

"You got something else you want to talk about, Frankie."

He blushed and turned a pretty shade of red. Then he seemed to change his mind and he stopped rocking.

"I wanted to tell you about Little Vinnie, Vinnie."

I knew Little Vinnie was not what he wanted to talk about, but if that was what he said then I had to let him wait until he was ready to tell me this other secret he was carrying around.

"What about Little Vinnie?"

"He's been going over to Pecan's place almost every night to gamble."

"WHAT!" It came out of me like a high pitched scream. "You knew this and you didn't tell me. Lacy mentioned the same thing to me when I left her in New York, but I thought she was lying to make me angry. And now you're telling me the same thing so I got to believe it." Then I let something slip I really didn't want to tell anyone.

"You know it was Jimmy Pecan who shot me when we were young over some dame I don't even remember. He got me right in my lower back. The bullet's been lodged there ever since, but it broke loose and the doctor thinks it's going to start traveling through my system. If it hits my heart, I'm dead. I'm a walking time bomb."

Frankie was stunned.

"You never told me."

"Nobody knows. I'm telling you now in case anything happens to me; you're in charge. I want you to take care of Rose, Little Vinnie—"

"—And Carmella, Vinnie?" He blushed again. What the fuck was wrong with him.

"Yeah, my pure little girl. As far as Little Vinnie goes, I think he's getting too big for his britches. Tonight, I want you to take him to the Miccosukee Casino and introduce him to Princess Snow Feather. That's her tourist name. She's

The Friggin' Altos
A Crime Family Gone Crazy

Chief Panther Bob's daughter and the manager. Make Little Vinnie Assistant Manager. That ought to keep him busy until I can put a scare into him about Pecan."

"Okay, boss, consider it done. When is Rose coming home?"

Rose, Rose, my poor half-blinded Rose. If she had been a horse she would have been glue.

"Not until after we take a shot at Pecan. So you cased The Blue Moon. Did you find any weak spots?

"Naw, it's pretty heavily guarded. The inside is nice—like back in The Thirties. A great band and a great singer."

"The Inferno is better. It's a lucky thing it was so easy to rebuild. Pecan's men are cross-eyed. It was easy to redo the damage."

Frankie's answer made my whole day gloomy.

"Except Rose's eyes."

"Yeah, except Rose's eyes."

"Ain't you going to call Brutto Demenza in."

"No. He's only for the big jobs."

Just like I asked Frankie he took Little Vinnie out to the Miccosukee Casino to introduce him to Princes Snow Feather and get him started working as the Assistant Manager. They were both craning their necks to find her.

"Okay, Little Vin, I'll find this doll, Princess Feather or something, and lay it out for her. Your father wants you to be Assistant Manager, learn the ropes and keep your act clean."

Little Vinnie was his same endearing self.

"Assistant Manager? What am I, the Vice President? Why not manager?

Frankie seemed to be the only person who could hold him in line.

"What are you so feaking hostile about? You're a nineteen-year-old punk with very little regard for your old man. Have you even been to see your mother in the hospital?"

"Yeah, yeah, but she was sleeping."

Frankie knew he was lying.

"You lie. She asked for you today because she hasn't had a visit from you. When you're through here haul your keister over to the hospital."

Then Little Vinnie spotted Princess Snow Feather.

"Hey, whose that vision in white over there?"

"That must be the Princess."

"Kiss me, I think I'm in love. Tell her the Assistant Manager is here."

So Frankie walks Little Vinnie over to the Princess.

The Friggin' Altos
A Crime Family Gone Crazy

"Princess Snow Feather, I want you to meet Little Vinnie Alto. He's your new Assistant Manager."

Frankie tells me the Princess is quite a dish, but she needs a lot of work on her attitude. She's got long black hair down to her waist and killing brown Bette Davis eyes.

"You must be Frankie. What have we here?" Her voice is like honey until she mentions my name. "Ah, the son of that crumb, Vinnie Alto. You know when my father bites the bullet, I'm going to be Chief and I'm going to get rid of all the crime bosses including Vinnie Alto. So this peach-cheek baby is sent to help me. What a fucken' joke." She laughed for a good minute. When she got her breath She looked at Vinnie with pity.

"Okay, okay. Your office is in the back of the hall. You'd do me a big favor if you never came out. If you do, just check the machines to make sure they aren't paying off too much. Leave the rest to me. When you learn to count maybe I'll trust you with the receipts." She took another long look in Little Vinnie's face and laughed as she strolled away. Then she did a strange thing. She stopped and turned to look at Little Vinnie again.

From that angle with her mouth shut she was a vision in a white ankle length Indian beaded gown with one pristine white eagle feather in her hair. She was a beauty all right, but like Long Loincloth had told me, a real bitch.

Little Vinnie just kept staring at her. Frankie felt sorry for the poor kid. He was way out of his depths. But, hey, a boy has to turn into a man sometime, and there's nothing like an abrasive broad to make him want to conquer her. Frankie could see the anger and humiliation on Little Vinnie's face, but he also saw something else in his eyes: raw hunger.

Meanwhile, I was over at Dante's Inferno auditioning dancers for the Strip Club. They were shaking it, bumping and grinding away. Since I had sent Ricco to the Hatitians, and Sammy Six Toes to the Cubans, my little gang was short some members. Trotsky had signed up three more from Jersey that morning. One was Dickie Blue; the other two were Charlie Coffee and Toots Feeney. Nice boys and hip. Dickie Blue was standing with me having a good time watching the strippers do their stuff. He seemed to be appreciating the raw talent.

"Boss, you got to pick four more dancers for the line up."

The Friggin' Altos
A Crime Family Gone Crazy

"See anything you like, Dickie Blue?"

"That little red head with the big bazooms might make my nights go better." Actually, he was lying.

"She's yours. You're one of the new boys, right?"

"Right. Me and two of my friends signed on this morning. By the way, there's a real looker asking to see you. A cool blond, and I mean cool."

"Bring her in. I could use a break."

And who comes gliding over: Marilyn, the mystery woman from the beach. I knew this was going to happen. Right away I know she's one of Pecan's guys and she's stalking me for a set up. But, that didn't keep me from appreciating the whole package. I had to admit, at times, Pecan had very good taste. She was a bombshell, and it was no joke that she looked like Marilyn Monroe right down to her T & A if you get my meaning. She brightened up my mood considerable. I was feeling giddy inside knowing I was going to taste this dainty morsel, and knowing she was as dangerous as a pit viper.

"Are you surprised to see me, Vinnie? I couldn't stay away. I need a job."

I thought it was a mediocre excuse, but what the hell did I care.

LaVerne and Sam Zocco

"You a stripper?" I made myself sound surprised and naïve.

She rumpled around her hips a little, licking her lip glossy with her saliva.

"Let me show you." She was good, she was very good.

"Not here," I say, "come to my office at ten o'clock. You can show me then."

And she did.

This is the kicker of all time.

Over at the Miccosukee Casino, Little Vinnie is roaming around the slot machines. It's two in the morning and he's feeling like a rag doll, but he ain't taking his eyes off the Princess whenever she pops into his line of vision. Then Frankie comes up to him.

"Watch those machines, Vin. Make sure they're not paying off too much. By the way there's some broad in your office to see you."

Little Vinnie is puzzled.

"A broad to see me? Hey, that sounds refreshing. I got to tell you the Princess is a guy in drag. She froze me right out. Still she ain't dog meat either."

Frankie shakes his head as Little Vinnie walks away. Little Vinnie disappears into his office where he finds, guess who? Marilyn is waiting for him leaning up against the desk all decked out in her stripper's outfit.

"You wanted to see me?" Little Vinnie nearly chokes on his spit.

"Jimmy Pecan says he's sorry about your mother. He wanted you to know it was all a terrible mistake. The boys who did it have paid the price."

She was smooth as glass.

And airhead Little Vinnie falls for it.

"I knew Jimmy wouldn't do such a thing to my mother. Who are you?"

"Just call me Marilyn. I'm a friend."

Then Little Vinnie realizes what she's wearing.

"Wow, is that a strip outfit you're wearing? It's two in the morning. You just get off a job or something?"

"I had a date at ten, but I'm free now. I came to audition for you."

Then Little Vinnie says the stupidest thing he will ever say in his life.

"Sorry, we don't put on a floor show."

But, Marilyn keeps plugging.

"I didn't say it was for a job. Lock the door."

And so he did.

LaVerne and Sam Zocco

Little Vinnie and me got a lot closer that night. It ain't everyday a son and his father eat off the same plate.

I was closing up the club. Frankie comes in so I asked him how it went with Little Vinnie, his first night.

"I think Little Vinnie found his calling. Some dame's got the hots for him."

That made me think there was hope for the kid yet. "About time. Where's Ricco?"

"He's over at the Port-a-Princes Haitian club."

"And how about Sammy Six Toes?"

"He's over at Salsa's Mambo club."

"We recruited some new boys in to fill in. Dickie Blue, Charlie Coffee, and Toots Feeney, all from Jersey. Where's my Camella?"

"She's with Rose at the hospital." There was that blush again.

"She's my angel—visits her mother—a good girl."

His blush got deeper. "Right," was all he said?

The Friggin' Altos
A Crime Family Gone Crazy

CHAPTER TEN

Now here's where we talk about Frankie and Carmella, and why he was always blushing lately when he was around me and I brought up the name of his goddaughter. I must have been blind with business, or suffering from my depression, or completely obsessed with killing Jimmy Pecan, not to have understood what was going on by observing Frankie's behavior. I guess my trust in Frankie made me believe he would never allow himself to fall in love with my daughter.

I thought, maybe, he would remember the Christmas Eve when I was rushing home to Rose and my two small children when I spotted this poor rag-a-muffin kid standing on the corner shaking with pneumonia. The new fallen snow covered his clothes and had soaked him through and through. He looked so frail in this big outsized overcoat from some shelter and he was hopping up and down to keep warm. He had no gloves on and he blew on his fingers that had already turned blue.

What could I do when he stuck out his shaking hand at me for some loose change? His face was dirty black and the rest of him was just as unwashed. I took one look at his handsome suffering face and knew I couldn't leave him there.

I didn't have to worry what Rose would say. When I walked in with this lanky, shy, sick kid, she looked from me to him and understood he was ours.

I never wanted Frankie in the rackets, but he followed me around where ever I went like a faithful dog who loved his master so much he couldn't stand to let me out of his sight. I didn't have the heart to shoo him away and as long as I let him tag along he was sure to learn exactly who I was and what my business was. The really sad thing is that Frankie was so smart I couldn't help listening to him and his good ideas. Whatever he told us worked. We made a fortune on the kid. The day he told me he wanted to be my enforcer I assigned him his first hit. You would have thought I was waiting in surgery to find out if he was going to live or die from some big operation, that's how nervous I was. I should have known, right there and then, the kid would carry the kill off with genius. He came back happy and excited. That night the boys and I drank to his health and gave him the respect he deserved for doing a man's job. From that moment on he had the job and my protection. None of the boys looked on him with envy. They knew Vinnie Alto had adopted a second son with all the power and wealth that went with it. Even though Frankie kept a low profile and never threw his weight around, the boys stood in awe of the skinny kid simply because his story was so miraculous. He had to be blessed to have touched me so deeply that there was genuine affection between him and me.

The kids loved him right off the bat. Little Vinnie had a big brother that kept an eye on him and was always keeping him in line. It wasn't Frankie's fault Little Vinnie grew up spoiled. His mother and I did that to him. But, it was because of Frankie, Little Vinnie never got malicious or into any big messes. Frankie was always there to smack him down or to tell me when I should step in before my son went too far with the boys. It had been Frankie who warned me that Little Vinnie was wading in dangerous waters hanging around Pecan, and I was going to take care of that.

As for Carmella, whenever Frankie was around there was no one else in the room. Frankie was the only one who could make her laugh until she dropped, or the only one to tease her about what a spoiled brat she was. He could even make her do homework.

Rose and I made him her honorary godfather with a big ceremony and party. She was twelve and he was nineteen. It was a reward for all his efforts in keeping her on the right path—he loved it and she loved it.

Who should be surprised that a strong bond sprang up between them? In my mind, the stronger the better. Frankie would always be around to protect her from herself where boys were concerned, even if I wasn't there. It never dawned on me it would be Carmella who would see Frankie as the object of her blossoming sexuality.

Even if she did, I always thought Frankie would have the good sense to look on it as infatuation and ignore it. I realize now I was pretty stupid where love was concerned.

Here's the scene with Frankie and Carmella that was going on while I was deep into plotting Jimmy Pecan's death. To tell you the truth Frankie was so busy carrying out my orders, I don't see how he had the energy. But there they were—parked at Dinner Key at midnight in my Lexus.

"Frankie you promised me you'd find someplace we can be alone. What are we doing at Dinner Key in Daddy's Lexus?"

Frankie was all agitated.

"Carmella, I'm trying to make a decision here."

The Friggin' Altos
A Crime Family Gone Crazy

"What decision?" As if she didn't know.

"If one night of hot steamy sex with a seventeen-year-old is worth dying for?"

"Is that the problem? Well, here, let me see if I can help you decide. Now you just sit there."

Now this is the part that makes a father squeamish, but it has to be told.

"Oh, Jeez. Oh Momma, Oh Daddy—(Frankie's moaning and groaning.) I must be in heaven because I see a bright white light."

Then there's a tapping on the window glass.

"Miami Police Officer, buddy. What's going on here? You want to get out of the car?"

Frankie's all confused not to mention worked up.

"Could you give me a minute officer?"

This cop was an okay guy.

"Oh, yeah, I see what you mean. Take your time."

Frankie gets rousted out of the car and he's standing humiliated and with terror in his heart.

"All right, you want to explain what's going on here before I run you into the Station?"

Well, you know how the politically correct cops are today. They ain't going to let no sex pervert go unless he's got a damn good reason.

"Sorry Officer, my friend and I just stopped to talk. You see I got a dilemma here. If I make love to her I know it will be a night of ecstasy. I also know if her father finds out I'll be dead before morning." He ain't about to tell the officer how old Carmella is.

"You got to be crazy. No broad is worth dying over. Seems it's a no-brainer. Give her the kiss-off right now while you're still in one piece. What's so difficult about that?" See the cop had it right.

"You want to tell her that, Officer? Just point your flashlight through the window."

It took the cop a few seconds to get the drift of Frankie's meaning. Then Carmella chimes in.

"Hi, Officer."

"Holy crap—you poor bastard. Prepare yourself—you're going to die."

With a shake of his head, and a wave of his baton, he sends them on their way. I think that shook up Frankie for a long time.

They were damn lucky they didn't get run into the station or I'd have found out about it and Frankie would have been dead.

I planned to visit Rose right along, but the restaurant and strip club was taking up a lot of my time. Besides, to tell the truth, seeing her in those

The Friggin' Altos
A Crime Family Gone Crazy

bandages made me feel like merda, and I blamed myself for what had happened. I knew I should have finished Pecan off before he ever got a toehold in Miami.

I couldn't go back and I couldn't go forward with that bastard still breathing. That was taking up most of my time. I didn't find out until later Trotsky, the traitor, was sneaking visits with Rose on the side. He was catching her at a very vulnerable time for her and making her think I didn't care two cents about what had happened to her. He never told her I was trying to get rid of Pecan for hurting her. I wouldn't have wanted her to know that, so see, I was painted as the bad guy. If you don't believe me here's the scene between Trotsky and Rose on one of his visits.

"Who's there?"

"It's me Rose, Ivan."

"Come in, sit on the bed. I thought it might have been Vinnie."

"He's very busy Rose with the club and the restaurant. You know how it is." What a lying fuck.

He gets Rose all upset.

She starts to cry and sob. "I'm so frightened for me and the children, Ivan. I may never see again." Now she's wailing.

LaVerne and Sam Zocco

This is when Ivan sees a small chance. He moves closer.

"Rose, Rose, please come away with me. We'll go away to a deserted island. I'll make you forget you ever heard of Vinnie Alto. Give me a chance, Rose. You know how I love you. Seeing you like this is torture. Vinnie is mad. He'll keep putting you and the children in danger. Please, Rose, say yes."

"I know what it's doing to the children. I'm afraid for all of us." Here's where Rose comes through. "But Vinnie would have to do such a terribly big crazy thing, that all that would be left to me is to leave. Please don't be disappointed, dear, dear, Ivan."

He still ain't giving up.

"I'm here for you, Rose. Anytime you can't deal with your life and want to change. I'm here."

"Wonderful, suffering, Ivan. Don't leave me."

"Oh, Rose."

Rose comes through again.

"But, please, take your hand off my thigh."

One thing I did make time for was giving Little Vinnie the scare of his life. I was going to make it so he would never go near The Blue Moon or Pecan again.

The Friggin' Altos
A Crime Family Gone Crazy

I'm sitting out on the terrace of the Alto mansion when Little Vinnie arrives in answer to my summons. There's the sound of happy little birds, and there's a sweet little squirrel climbing the palm tree right in front of the patio.

"Papa, you wanted to see me? What a beautiful garden. The birds singing, and that little squirrel playing."

"Yes, my son, sit, sit. You know I used to think you were just slow, but now I'm convinced you're an idiot."

Little Vinnie sits there stunned and hurt.

"Papa, why are you saying such hurtful things to me? What have I done?"

When I start talking you can see the terror creep into his eyes.

"Is it true you been going over to The Blue Moon to gamble and hang out with Jimmy Pecan? The man who blinded your mother—the man who would do anything to see me dead?"

Vinnie sinks into his chair.

"He said he was sorry. Besides you treat me like a retard. Jimmy treats me like a man."

That's when I bring up my gun and shoot that cute, innocent squirrel right off the tree. The thing exploded into fur and air.

Vinnie went white as a sheet.

"Holy merda, you killed that squirrel." He starts crying. "A sweet, innocent little squirrel."

I put my face right up to his. I can smell the tic-tacs.

"If I hear one more time you went to the Blue Moon, I'm going to leave you pene-less. You know what Pene means in Italian—PENIS! YOU NUMB NUT. NOW GO AHEAD AND TRY ME."

"I'm sorry Papa. I guess you'll never be proud of me. A poor innocent little squirrel."

My heart was hardened because of Rose.

"Take that blubbering outside."

Poor Frankie, he must have been going crazy the day I called him in to find out what he found out from bugging Jimmy Pecan's house.

"Vinnie, you're never going to believe this. I did what you told me to do. I broke into Jimmy Pecan's house and bugged the hell out of it. I watched him for a week."

"That crazy psycho. He's a friggin' menace. Shooting my club up, maybe blinding Rose."

"It was a freakin' genius idea of yours to find out what he loves most so we can whack it. How'd you think that up?"

I hadn't told Frankie about the ghost of Al Capone.

"Just popped into my head. What did you find out? Look at me I'm all anxious and shaking to find out. Did you find out what he loves most?"

"Yeah, but it's weird."

"Well we're dealing with a really weird guy. All right already, tell me who or what is it? Whoever it is, we make our plans and we hit Pecan where his soul is. If it's his nightclub, We'll destroy it—if it's his mistress—we'll take care of her. Someone told me everyone has a secret thing that would drive them crazy if they lost it. Okay, so who do we spadosh?"

Frankie starts to laugh so hysterically he's got me joining in.

"Quit screwing around, Frankie, you're making my stomach ache. Come on, come on, before I croak you, tell me. What does Jimmy Pecan love more than life itself."

IT'S A BIRD! A white talking bird with golden feathers on its head. Get this he calls it Lover Boy!"

"Nooo, that's it, a friggin' bird?"

"Not just any bird, Vinnie. Jimmy Pecan tells him all his secrets. They carry on regular conversations—it's like the bird is giving Pecan advice."

I'm thinking of Al Capone and how he gives me advice. I make up my mind right then and there.

"KIDNAP THE BIRD!" I'm dead serious.

Frankie leans in like he didn't hear me right.

"What."

"Kidnap the bird, I said."

"Okay, Vin. Maybe you're right. Pecan tells this bird everything. It's like he's in love with the damn thing, you know like that little bulldozer you carry around."

Then his eyes screw up in horror.

"You're not going to cut the bird's head off and stick it in Pecan's bed, are you?"

I give him a slap up the side of the head.

"Just do what I tell you. Get the bird."

The Friggin' Altos
A Crime Family Gone Crazy

CHAPTER ELEVEN

You won't believe how nervous I was waiting for Frankie to come home with that bird. I was pacing back and forth thinking that Pecan had to be crazier than I was if he was in love with a bird and used it to confide in.

Wasn't that loonier than having a ghost from the twenties giving you advice and helping you with your depression? Then the truth dawned: we were both nuts.

For a long time now I had a suspicion that just being a crime boss was the height of lunacy. I mean when you get right down to it look at what you're doing with your life. You're murdering people for profit. Not only that, but you're dragging other people into this mad world and they're doing the dirty jobs. You're corrupting everyone around you and they don't seem to mind at all. It could be the feeling of superiority that makes them feel invincible, or maybe they understood once you were in there was no way out.

Hey, I'm talking about church-going people here with families. Aren't they ever fearful of losing their souls? In my own case I never really thought about right or wrong until that bullet broke loose. So I have to admit I said a few prayers to myself, and Rose forced me to accompany her to the big cathedral, but after that I started thinking what I could do to beat the rap. I was thinking a lot about that those days. I told you a criminal always thinks he's got a way to beat the system and I was looking awfully hard for a way to overcome death. My odds were pretty high, but that didn't stop me from trying.

So here I was pacing around then Frankie appears with the huge golden cage with a green towel thrown over it that said St. Andrews Golf Course. I told you Pecan was a classy guy.

Frankie came bounding in the room and offered the cage to me.

"Here's the bird, Vinnie. Beautiful ain't he?"

He was making screeching and parrot sounds, but nothing that sounded like a human word. He was beautiful though. This bird must have set Pecan back a large pile of "K" notes. Maybe twenty if the bird could really hold a conversation. I was impressed with the bird's size and feathers, white like velvet all around, and gold like a kingly crown on top his head.

"Wow, what a beautiful bird." I called to him. "Polly want a cracker? Pretty bird, say hello, say hello."

The Friggin' Altos
A Crime Family Gone Crazy

And what pops out of this bird's mouth.

"Screw you. Where's Jimmy? Where's Jimmy?"

I'm knocked back on my heels.

"I'll be damned—he's a riot."

Frankie says with supreme pride, "His name's Lover Boy."

So I give it another shot.

"Hey, Lover Boy—say Hi, Vinnie—say I love you Vinnie."

The bird blinks his tiny black eyes at me and cocks his head like he's really listening. Then he lets fly.

"Vinnie Alto's a pimp. Vinnie Alto's a pimp. Lover Boy wants a BJ, Vinnie."

Frankie had to grab my arms from out of the cage.

"Vinnie, you're strangling him. Get your hand out of the cage."

"That bastard Pecan taught him that. Ouch, the son-of-a-bitch bit me! Get a bird handler. I want to know what he knows about Jimmy Pecan. Hey, Lover Boy, tell me about Jimmy, your boyfriend."

The bird actually spit through the bars of his cage.

"Screw you!"

LaVerne and Sam Zocco

The next day I was at my psychiatrist's office for some special tests Dr. Ruth has conjured up. She was looking luscious as ever but she had her tortoise shell glasses on and that's when I knew she meant business. She was going to get a little mouthy today too.

"Well, Vinnie, where's Al Capone? I thought you were going to bring him in for a session."

"Don't get your pantyhose in a twist, he's going to come. Right now, he's slapping around a bird."

She sucked on the stem of the right side of her glasses.

"I don't even want to go there, Vinnie. I just want to do a little test today."

"Ink spots?"

"In a way. It'll give me more information about you. What I want you to do is tell me the names of three people, living or dead, that you think should have holidays named after them, and three names of people you think should never have been born."

I know I frowned. Whenever I'm called upon to really dig down I feel like my brain is on fire and I'm smelling smoke.

"Hey, that takes some thinking. Come on over here and help me clear my mind. Really, doc, why don't you try some Vinnie Love, you might like it?

She wasn't buying.

"Just give me the names, and before you ask, you can't use yourself."

"Okay, doc. Here's my three names of people I think should have a holiday named after them. First John Travolta."

"And why is that?"

"Because he's Italian."

She scribbled away on that stupid note pad she always has on her lap. "Tell me another name."

"Well, then there's Joe Pesci."

She laughs at this cause she thinks she sees how this is going.

"Why, Mr. Pesci?"

"Because he's Italian."

Again with the scribbling.

"Okay, one more."

"Well, of course it has to be Joe DiMaggio."

She thinks she's so fucken' smart.

"Don't tell me—because he's Italian?"

"Are you crazy? I picked Joe because he's the greatest baseball player that ever lived. You're not very quick on the uptake, are you, doc? So am I crazy?"

"No, but you're very ethnocentric."

"Yeah, I know a lot about electricity."

"Now, you have to tell me the three people you think should never have been born."

I squinted up my eyes like I was taken a dump.

"Okay, okay. Don't rush me, I'm thinking."

Twenty minutes later I'm still thinking.

"Vinnie, you've been thinking twenty minutes. Who are the three people you think should never have been born?"

"Okay, I'm ready."

"Well?"

"First, Jimmy Pecan."

"The man who shot up your restaurant? That's understandable."

"He hurt Rose."

Her comment surprised me.

"You love your wife?"

I was flabbergasted. "Of course I love my wife. And then there's Tony Sweets. He was my ex-partner. He ratted me out.

We was childhood hoodlums together."

"So you value loyalty."

"Sure, don't you? And the third person who never should have been born was my father!"

She jumped in disbelief.

"Vinnie! Your father. Why?"

"Because he died too young. Just when I needed him the most he took a powder."

The Friggin' Altos
A Crime Family Gone Crazy

"He couldn't help it Vinnie."

"Yeah, I know. Give me a tissue. Jeez, what a stupid test."

I spent the next hour spilling my guts to Dr. Ruth.

When I got back to the Mansion Frankie came up from the cellar where he and the bird handler had been working the bird over.

"Okay, Frankie. What did you and Al get out of the bird? You give him a good going over?"

Frankie looked a little confused when I mentioned Al Capone. Again, I hadn't told anyone I was seeing the old gangster's ghost. After the day I had with my psychiatrist I wasn't in the mood to share any more information from the soul of Vinnie Alto. She made me think back to my father and how it felt when he died. I still couldn't stem the tears that were in my eyes. I never realized his death had hit me so hard, or how much anger I carried around that he left me right when I needed him the most. She finally made me deal with all those feelings. I got to tell you it made me feel light as a feather to have all that baggage taken off my shoulders. I just wanted you to know there is some relief in seeing a shrink.

Frankie, of course, knew none of this.

"Sure, Vinnie, but who the hell is Al? You losing it or what?"

"Shut your face. Just tell me what happened with the frigging bird?"

"I hired the bird handler like you said. The bird sang like a canary."

"Just what I want to hear. Did he also teach the bird what I said to teach him?"

"Yeah."

"Okay, bring him up here and get Pecan on the phone."

It took him a while to get the bird back in the cage, but when Frankie brought the bastard up, he dials Pecan's number and Pecan himself answers. It's the first time I talk to Pecan since he shot me. It was like electricity going through me to hear the voice of the man who had made my life hell and hurt Rose.

"This is Pecan. What?"

It was like a blast from the past hearing that same whiny voice I remembered so well.

He was still the same uncouth guy. I put the bird up to the phone and prompted him to repeat to Pecan what the handler had been teaching him for two days.

"They're torturing me, Papa! Come get your Lover Boy. Hurry, hurry!"

The Friggin' Altos
A Crime Family Gone Crazy

It was my turn to turn the screw tighter.

"You friggin' weirdo. You blinded Rose. You want your bird, meet me at the Hollywood Dog Races. Just you and me, no bodyguards. He's told us everything. Get it pal, everything!"

The bird chimes in right on cue.

"I love you Vinnie Alto—I love you."

Pecan sounds like a broken man when he moans.

"Lover Boy, what have they done to you?" It's just like Al said it got him right in the soul.

When I hang up I can't shut Frankie up about this bird.

"This sucker is a smart son-of-a-bitch. He gave us the combination to Pecan's safe at The Blue Moon. He told us Pecan sleeps in a pink nightgown and that he's got a new mistress. He also told me about the plight of the parrots being brought into the country illegally. We should do something about that."

"You really are a bonehead, you know that?"

"You really going to bring that bird back to Pecan at the dog races?"

"Yeah, I said no bodyguards and I mean no bodyguards. This is family honor."

"But, Vinnie, the guy's psycho. You think he's going to meet you fair and square?"

LaVerne and Sam Zocco

"Let's ask the bird. Hey, Lover Boy, will Pecan meet me at the races with no bodyguards?

"Screw you."

What a bird.

Frankie is all hipped up now. "Vinnie, even if Pecan's there without his bodyguards at the races, how you going to take your revenge? He'll be looking for a trick."

I have to laugh at Frankie sometimes. He's a sharp mind when it comes to scamming but when it comes to having real imagination; well he's a little short.

"Frankie you got no freakin' imagination. What's the first thing he's going to do when I give him Lover Boy?"

"If he's so freaky about that parrot, he'll probably kiss him."

"Bingo! So all we do is put some fast acting poison around the bird's beak and Pecan buys the farm."

I'm laughing for the first time in two days.

"But, won't that kill the parrot too?"

"What the hell do we care—we get Jimmy Pecan and Rose is revenged."

Frankie seems devastated.

"He's such a smart bird—it seems a shame to kill him."

The Friggin' Altos
A Crime Family Gone Crazy

I'm flabbergasted.

Well here's what happened when the night came for us to take the bird and meet Pecan at the Hollywood Dog Track. He's sitting in his private box like a king but without bodyguards. If you don't believe it there is honor amongst thieves.

"Pecan."

"Vinnie."

"Here's your bird."

Then the bird don't behave. Why didn't I think that the one flaw in the plan was that the damn bird could talk."

"NO, NO, PAPA, DON'T KISS ME. DO YOU BELIEVE THIS STUPID TURNIP HEAD? HE PUT FAST-ACTING—"

I fire one round from the gun in my sock. I lied. No honor among thieves. "HE GOT ME PAPA, HE GOT ME."

Pecan is yelling and screaming like he got hit. He's crying and carrying on grabbing the bird.

'HE KILLED MY BIRD! PLEASE DON'T DIE, MY KISSES WILL SAVE YOU."

Just what I want he's kissing the bird all over its beak.

The bird can't believe it.

"You're as friggin' stupid as Vinnie is. Viva Liberte, Papagayo.!"

Then this Irish cop comes running up.

"What's going on here?" He has this thick Irish brogue.

I play it cool and innocent.

"That guy just fell over when I was talking to him. I think he's hurt officer. Look, his lips are moving, he wants to tell you something."

"Jeez, it's Jimmy Pecan. What are you trying to say, Mr. Pecan?"

Pecan is squirming on the ground with the poison in him. He can hardly talk or breathe.

"Put Lover Boy in my hand."

The cop looks at him as though he's crazy.

"He's dying and he's talking dirty. Someone call for an ambulance. Hey, where'd those two guys go with that big white parrot?"

Then I hear Lover Boy from far away. He's weak but he still manages. "Screw you."

I learn they took Pecan to the same Hospital Rose is in, and of all things put him in the room right next to hers. But there are so many guards around; it's like an army. I know if he lives, I'll have to try again when I can get him in my power.

When I get home there's Frankie waiting for me.

"Frankie, why did you bring home that friggin' bird?"

The Friggin' Altos
A Crime Family Gone Crazy

"It was just a flesh wound, Vinnie, in his wing. The bird handler begs you give the bird to him. He pumped his stomach of the poison. He will live and he's so beautiful—let him have him."

"All right all ready, and good riddance. Just get rid of him. Now, come on, we got to go and get Rose at the Hospital."

"Too bad they saved Pecan's life. I just called in, he's going to make it." This news makes me grab my head where a mother of a headache has started.

"I almost feel like calling in Brutto Demenza." Frankie moans.

"Ah, Vinnie, not Brutto Demenza. Not yet."

I give in quickly. If you'd ever seen Brutto Demenza you'd understand.

"Maybe you're right. This ain't big enough for Brutto Demenza. By the way, I want to speak to Ricco, Sammy Six Toes, Little Vinnie and my mother. I want to check up on all of them. I've been letting it slide with everything that's been going on. Remind me."

"Sure, boss, I'll remind you tomorrow."

CHAPTER TWELVE

Finally the day came when I brought Rose from the hospital. She still had those ugly bandages across her eyes, and I still felt guilty especially when she kept walking into walls. But, I can't tell you how my heart sang to be able to kiss her again, and give her a little feel now and again. She didn't seem to be inclined to tell me that Trotsky had been hanging around, and I didn't ask. Deep in my heart I knew Rose would never leave me unless I did something so terrible, that she couldn't forgive me. Oh, I had already done a million things that could have qualified for that, but I always made it a point never to tell Rose anything about my business.

"Rose, honey, how you feeling?"

"Good, Vinnie. It's good to be home from the hospital."

"I'm sorry I didn't come as often as I should, but I was so busy getting the club all repaired and hiring singers and dancers. But, now I'm all yours. Give us a kiss."

"You'll have to kiss me Vinnie. Remember, I can't see."

"Oh, yeah, I forgot."

The Friggin' Altos
A Crime Family Gone Crazy

Then comes this voice from the end of the bed.

"Vinnie, would you two mind moving over a little, it's crowded down here." It was Al Capone.

I thought Rose was going to have kittens.

"Vinnie, who's that at the end of our bed?"

It was my turn to be amazed.

"You mean you heard Al? No. What did he just say?"

"He said that we should move because it was too crowded down there at the end of the bed."

'THAT'S RIGHT!" I was astounded and out of my mind with joy. "You mean you hear Al Capone too, Rose?"

"I most certainly do, and if this is a joke, it's not a very funny one."

I kissed her all over her face.

"You don't understand, Rose. I thought I was going crazy seeing Al Capone. But, now you hear him too, which means if your eyes weren't practically shot out, you could see him too. Is that right, Al?"

The Italian accent was so romantic.

"Yes, that's right. Now Mrs. Alto don't get scared. See I'm here to help Vinnie with his business decisions. I'm also supposed to see to it that you both don't get hurt until you're stable again?

LaVerne and Sam Zocco

Rose was fascinated.

"You mean you're hear like a guardian angel to watch and see we don't get hurt—(it dawned on her) you mean, Vinnie and I are both crazy?"

"That's it. But don't worry, as soon as you both are sane again, I'll just disappear."

"And how soon will that be?" She was always the practical one, my Rose.

"Maybe never."

I may be insane, I may never come out of it, but I can tell you making love with a ghost at the bottom of the bed is really nuts.

The next morning Frankie was right there to remind me to get Ricco, Six Toes, Little Vinnie and Mom on the phone to check up on them. The first one I called was Ricco.

He was speaking from the Haitian nightclub, Port-a-Princes.

"Ricco, its Vinnie. How you making out down there at the Port-a-Princes?"

"Mon, it's so fine, Mon."

"What's wrong with your voice?"

"What you say, Mon? I speak only the Creole, Mon."

"Everything okay over there?"

The Friggin' Altos
A Crime Family Gone Crazy

"Oh Mon, paradise is mine, Mon. Sweet brown ladies, so fine, moon, Rum Collins all the day, Mon., throwing the dice, sweet Mon."

"You want to come home, Mon.?"

"The gig is swinging Mon., leave me be, Mon. Adieu, Mon."

I must have roared at Frankie cause he nearly fell off his chair.

"Get Ricco the hell out of there before he joins the Ton Ton Macoot." Frankie was out the door.

The next call was to Sammy Six Toes at Salsa's Mambo club.

"Sammy, how you doing over there with Salsa?"

"I am King of the Mambo, Senor. Mucho Gusto my white shirt with the frilly sleeves shows my chest off. My tight black pants drive the Senoritas muy loco. I dance the Samba, rumba, tango, y esta noche; I win the Mambo contest. Ole!"

I rubbed my hand across my face hard.

"Ah, Sammie. Have you lost your friggin' mind. You paying attention to our share of the take?"

"Marie Elena say I am pretty like the strong bull. Ah, Toro! Si, caliente mujer, dance all night, love all day. Adios."

LaVerne and Sam Zocco

I waited for Frankie to get home with Ricco, then had him stand by the phone to listen to the rest of the calls while I gave him instructions.

"Get Sammy Six Toes back here before he joins the Cuban Paramilitary Brigade in the Everglades."

The next call was to Little Vinnie out at the Miccosukee Casino.

"Little Vinnie, how you making out with Chief Panther Bob?"

"My tourist name now, "Big Moccasins." I sit in the sauna smoking the bong pipe. I see visions."

"Jeez, not you too? Where's Chief Panther Bob?"

"Chief Panther Bob is very sick. Walgreen say he has ulcer. Tonight, Princess Snow Feather sits in council, smoke much bong pipe. She is going to whip into downtown Miami and burn down the Port-a-Princes, the Mambo Club and Dante's Inferno."

"Get him out of there, Frankie. There's trouble on the reservation."

Finally, I made one last call to my mother, Frances.

"Vinnie! My little bubbala—I'm so mishoggina—I'm in my schemata—I'm late for Schul."

The Friggin' Altos
A Crime Family Gone Crazy

"Who is this?"

"It's momma, Vinnie. I'm in my condo on Miami Beach. Oi Vey, you're such a putz. Why you no call your Momma? What have I done to deserve such a bad son? Rabbi Lieberman says I expect too much. I got to go now. Tonight its Mah Jong, and bingo. Shalom, Vinnie."

"Oh, God. Frankie get over there and get ma. Then bring all four back to the Mansion. We got to deprogram them. We also got trouble brewing on the reservation. I got to warn, Overlord Pierre, Lazaro, and Chief Panther Bob. Now, hurry. And get rid of that bird."

"Screw you." For a minute I thought it was Frankie who said that but no it was that damn bird.

Hours later Frankie came home with the news along with Ricco, Sammy, Little Vinnie and Ma.

"I was just in time, Vinnie. Princess Snow Feather has gone mad. She and her council have burnt down the Port-a-Princes, the Mambo Club, and they were just on their way to Dante's Inferno. They also tore down the Seminole Flag from the City Hall. Crazy Joe, The Generalissimo of Miami blames it all on you for coming to Florida. He says no way your getting a liquor license."

I was so relieved and so crazy.

"Why didn't they burn down Dante's Inferno? What stopped them?"

"Chief Panther Bob got up out of his sick bed and announced a freebie night at the casino. All the police disappeared out to the casino. Then he took away the bong pipe from Snow Feather. The council only follows the one with the bong pipe. It's all quiet now."

I was able to drop in a chair for a minute and wipe the sweat from my face.

"I wish I had been able to see it all."

Rose chimes in. "Me too."

Then something dawns on me.

"How come they let Jimmy Pecan's place alone."

Frankie makes a guess.

"I think maybe Pecan and Snow Feather got something going, although it seems to me she's got the eye for Little Vinnie."

"And this Generalissimo of Miami, is not going to give us a liquor license but already gave one to Pecan? What is he, potsa?"

Frankie laughed.

"They don't call him Crazy Joe for nothing."

Now I get all my family into the front room.

"Quiet, I got something to say to all of you."

The Friggin' Altos
A Crime Family Gone Crazy

There is suddenly massive silence as the talking dies down.

"Ricco, you're not Haitian. Sammy, you're not Cuban. Ma, you're not Jewish, and Little Vinnie; you're not Miccosukee. We got real trouble coming from The Generalissimo of Miami. Riccco, Sammy, Little Vinnie, and Ma, you're going to stay here until you're deprogrammed. I'm sending Dickie Blue and the others to take your places. Now anybody got anything to say?"

"Oi Vey."

"Mon, oh, Mon."

"Carumba!"

"Whose got the bong pipe?"

"Screw you."

CHAPTER THIRTEEN

The very next day I go over to see Chief Panther Bob to see how the old boy is doing. He's sitting up in bed in his multi-million dollar mansion that touches on the Casino property. For as far as the eye can see there's forests and rivers, and a private airport where his Lear Jet is waiting. I pass two very beefy bodyguards on my way in, and they search me like they ain't had a date in a month. They finally grunt me through. Chief Panther Bob who sounds just like Jack Nicholson greets me.

"My eyes welcome you, Vinnie Alto."

Well, wouldn't Jack greet me the same way? And he's not Miccosukee.

I join into the spirit of the thing.

"My heart jumps for joy to see you are well again, Chief. I was very worried that Princess Snow Feather would have her way, and start a war between our families."

"Princess Snow Feather has been sent for punishment to Big Woman with ugly stick."

"Little Vinnie—tourist name Big Moccasins—has seen the error of his ways also."

The Friggin' Altos
A Crime Family Gone Crazy

"Too much bong pipe mixed with fire water often make one feel powerful and can lead to craziness of the spirit. How about the Heat—you know basketball? I thought maybe you liked it."

"Yeah, I love it. I brought Dickie Blue to take over for Little Vinnie. Please chief, don't ever die."

"And you, Vinnie Alto, stay well and healthy. Let's go over to my sauna where we can talk privately."

I couldn't help laughing.

"What, no sweat lodge?"

"Only when tourists are around."

I got to tell you the sauna, with its dry heat was an improvement over the sweat lodge. Panther Bob sat down and threw a pan of water over the hot rocks and the steam filled the air and made me cough. After a while it felt very good on my naked body.

"It is good, Vinnie Alto, to sit naked and let the heat of many suns cleanse your body and soul."

"Can we talk while we're cleansing Chief?"

"Of course. What is it you wish to talk about?"

"My man, Sammy Six Toes says we are having troubles getting a liquor license from the city of Miami. I come to wise chief to tell me what I must do to make the city understand without a liquor license my club, Dante's Inferno, cannot open."

The chief nodded his head up and down.

"It is not the city that holds you captive—it's The Generalissimo of Miami."

I was befuddled and bemused.

"What's this guy got to do with the licensing department giving me the liquor license? Don't I just pay the fee, add a little schmooze money to grease the wheels?"

"My son, the Mayor wears a Generalissimo uniform with a large blue sash and many medals. He rides a white horse around town, and he has his own palace guard who surround City Hall."

"Potsa, huh?"

"Precisely. Crazy but powerful."

"Listen, Chief, tell me about the city of Miami? What area are we talking about?"

"South to Key Largo, North to Little River, East to the ocean, and West to Tamiami Trail."

I whistled through the steam.

"Hey, that's big territory. So the Generalissimo owns the license department?"

"Yes. And all the government jobs."

"How about the courts?"

"They belong to The general."

"What about the newspapers?"

The Friggin' Altos
A Crime Family Gone Crazy

The Miami Herald is his."

"Schools, hospitals, police department, fire department?"

"All."

"So he's got a right to be crazy with power. What your saying is I gotta see The General—and speak to him in plain English."

"No, plain Spanish."

"Let me see if I have this straight. If I want to get a liquor license, I got to see this Generalissimo?"

"You speak true."

"Do I make an appointment at City Hall?"

"You can. But a gringo will sit there all day. Sorry, I don't know the Cuban term for poor white bastard, only Mexican."

"You got to be kidding me."

"No kidding when in sauna."

"Well, what do you think I should do?"

"You go ahead and open Dante's Inferno without a liquor license. The General will find you."

That made me feel better. "Throw some more water on the stones, Chief. I'm starting to relax."

The chief lifted his hand to pour more water on the hot stones, when he peered through the sauna window. He wiped the steam away.

"Ah, here comes Princess Snow Feather now."

"What's her real name. You know, the one not for the tourists."

"Real name, Adam Billy."

"Her too? But the warrior she sent to my house, Long Loincloth, is also named Adam Billy."

"Very few pale faces know. We all named Adam Billy by horse soldiers who came from great white chief in Washington to settle us on our reservation. Not very imaginative, we're they?"

"Hold it, hold it. I'm naked here. She allowed in the Sauna?"

"No, but she come to apologize. Put these flip-flops over your Willy. She will never notice. Enter Snow Feather. You have something to say to our friend, Vinnie Alto?"

"Wow, it's hot in here. I'm sorry about getting Big Moccasins involved with the bong pipe. I have big shame for causing trouble and have asked my father for forgiveness, and humbly ask your forgiveness. However, when my father goes to the great white hunting ground, me and Jimmy Pecan are going to kick your Italian ass."

"How dare you shame me. Vinnie Alto and I are at peace. He's a good man and knows many things."

The Friggin' Altos
A Crime Family Gone Crazy

She looked at me with pity on her face. Her dark brown eyes starred at me intensely.

"There is one big secret Vinnie Alto is blind to. Are you tough enough to listen to the truth, white man."

I was about to stand up to face her when I remembered my bare Willy. "Vinnie Alto is tough as steel. Go ahead; give it to me straight. What's the big secret I should know?"

When it came spilling out of her mouth I was completely unprepared for her venom.

"Your beloved enforcer, Frankie, has been boffing your seventeen-year-old daughter, Carmella. Oh, gross you dropped your flip-flops."

When I came to I was in the chiefs mansion with him standing over me.

"Where am I? Where am I?"

"You are in my wigwam. You fainted from the heat of the sauna."

He was like me. He didn't know which world he fit into.

"No, no, I remember. Where's that little snot you call a daughter?"

"I have sent her back to Big Woman with ugly stick."

"Did I hear her right? Did she say Frankie, my enforcer, my friend—" I began crying.

LaVerne and Sam Zocco

"—has been doing horizontal rain dance with your daughter, Carmella."

"No, no, not Frankie—not with my sweet innocent Carmella—my pure flower."

"She's slut now."

"Forgive me for leaving, chief, I'm outta here."

I was way down the drive and never even heard him calling after me. "But, you are still naked. Too late, he is gone."

I heard about this later. Snow Feather comes back to the house when I'm running down the drive. Chief Panther Bob is really upset with her.

"Adam Billy, why you lie and tell that poor man his seventeen-year-old daughter is no longer pure?"

She sneered like a cougar.

"He spoiled my plans to take over Miami by taking Big Moccasins away from me. Little Vinnie hates his father. He has the makings of another Tiger Jim, The Roadrunner."

The chief couldn't believe his ears.

"You were lying when you said Frankie had beat on Carmella's tom tom."

"Of course I was lying. He's going to murder Frankie now."

"Of this you are proud? He was still naked from the sauna."

She sneers again.

"What kind of father goes into hysterics over his daughter's sex life?"

"He who has love in his heart for her the same as I have for you. You have cared for no man since Wily Coyote, the crocodile, ate Tiger Jim. I think you love Little Vinnie."

"You speak like an old woman. It is Jimmy Pecan I'm interested in. Besides, Little Vinnie has a blonde stripper who comes to see him every night. She has his heart."

"I think I see green God of jealousy in your eyes."

"It's the sauna. It makes my father's eyes fuzzy."

CHAPTER FOURTEEN

To tell you the truth I don't remember a thing coming home in the car, except how it would feel to put my hands around Frankie's neck and choke him to death. Remember, I wasn't in on the gag that Princess Snow Feather was playing on me. All I was thinking about was Frankie taking my baby to a motel and having his way with her. You may think I was aware that I was completely nude, but I was so numb I didn't even wonder why the cross-breeze was making me shiver.

I drove that Lexus for all I was worth. Down State-Road 44l, over to AIA then down to the causeway and over to Palm Island. All the time I'm slapping away tears from my eyes, some for me, some for Carmella, and some for Frankie for old-times sake. Incensed beyond measure, I swirled that great car through the gate onto the estate right up to the front door. I slammed that heavy door like I had Frankie's Willy caught in between the edge of the door and the door lock. And I went running up the long flat steps into the pink mansion with never a care for what I would run into.

The Friggin' Altos
A Crime Family Gone Crazy

Ricco was standing in the hall with his mouth gaping as I came through the door.

"Hey, boss, you're naked."

"And Ricco, you're ugly. Where the rotten stinking hell is Frankie?"

Ricco was coughing and making funny motions with his head toward the front room.

"Are you having a fit or what?"

Ricco cleared his throat. "Frankie took Carmella shopping over to the Gap."

I laughed high and painfully.

"Yeah, I'll just bet. I want you to go out after them now, and drag them back here, and don't take no excuses."

"Sure, boss, only don't you think you ought to say hello to your mother and her bridge club?"

And there in the front room, for God and everyone to see, were four old ladies sitting around a card table, all with cards sticking in their hands. And me with my Willie hanging.

"Sorry, ladies," I groaned. "I just came from the Sauna out at the Miccosukee casino. Don't pay me any mind. Just go on with your game."

I kinda bent forward and backed out of the doorway but my mother wouldn't let me go. I guess mother's just don't notice when their sons are naked.

"Vinnie, dear, this is Sister Jeanne, the President of Barry College."

I gave the impartial turncoat a jaunty salute and ran like hell up the stairs.

My mother watched me fly with a look of concern on her face. "Sorry, Sister. What did you bid?"

"One thick club. Is it hot in here, or is it just me?"

I ran into my bedroom ranting and raving, pacing like a tiger, anxious to see my sweet Carmella, and beat the hell out of Frankie.

Rose knew immediately something was wrong.

"Vinnie, calm down. You know I can't see since you caused my eyes to be practically shot out."

I was in such pain I could barely control my voice.

"Sorry, Rose. I'm a lunatic—I feel sick inside. My stomach is burning—I've puked all the way home—and I'm naked."

"So you found out about Frankie and Carmella?"

"You knew, you knew, and you didn't tell me? I had to find it out from that Miccosukee Napoleon. She said, (I was hardly able to say it) Frankie—my beloved Frankie—has—how can I

The Friggin' Altos
A Crime Family Gone Crazy

say this politely—bought Carmella her own lamp post to lean on. No, has sold her to a man named Jerome. No, has inserted—copulated—peeked into her panty drawer."

"Are you trying to say Frankie and Carmella have had sexual relations?"

That made me cry all the harder.

"That's it. You know what this means. It means cutting Frankie the traitor and leaving him in a remote place to bleed to death. Where's my pen knife?"

"You can't mean your going to pull that old Italian ritual of carving a "T" into the cheek of a traitor? That went out with cement overshoes. Isn't that right, Al?"

From the foot of the bed, "Yeah, that's right. That's how I got this scar on my cheek."

"Who says I'm going to carve it in his cheek?"

"Oh, God, Vinnie, now control yourself. I hear Frankie and Carmella coming up the stairs."

The minute Frankie steps over the threshold I have him pinned up against the wall. Carmella screams, which in turn makes Ricco scream.

"All right, Frankie. You see this knife—if you give me the wrong answer, I will carve the "T" in your cheek for traitor. You bastard, have you been touching Carmella's pee-pee? Watch how you answer, cause you'll leave a long trail of blood from here out to a remote place to bleed to death."

"Ah, boss," Ricco chimes in, "nobody bleeds to death anymore." My hand thrust out like a cobra and Ricco's hand is bleeding all over the floor.

Frankie seems to be relieved. "Oh, God, my day has come. Vinnie, I swear I never touched the untouched Carmella. But, she's been manhandling me pretty good. I love her Vinnie. I know I'm scum, but I love her. I've been waiting until next month when she turns eighteen to ask her to marry me. But, I'm glad you know it now. I'm sorry Vinnie. I should have told you. Cut away if you want. I couldn't help myself. Look at those breasts, those long sexy legs—"

Ricco is looking a little woozy. "Can someone get me a towel and some liniment."

"Shut up." I'm trying hard but everyone else seems so unconcerned I think they're all loony.

"Vinnie, I swear to you I wanted to but I never touched her. If you want me to leave I'll go, but it's up to Carmella if she wants to come with me. Why don't we leave it up to her?"

I drop into a chair. Everyone's being too cool about the whole thing to suit me.

"Okay, let's ask Carmella. Baby, what have you got to say?"

The Friggin' Altos
A Crime Family Gone Crazy

She ain't the least bit shy.

"Daddy, if there's a "B" for "Boring" in the Italian revenge please cut it into Frankie and let me watch. The guys dead and don't know it. I should know I've been teasing him for months now and his thing ain't moved yet. He's the all time straight arrow with a dead shaft. It's been snoozeville. My plans are all made. Me and my friend Beverly are going out on the road. I want to be a singer and she wants to be a prostitute. We're going solo. With our boobs and our innocence we'll make millions."

Rose hears this big crashing noise.

"God, what was that ungodly noise?"

"Daddy passed out, and yuck he's naked."

"Rose, this is Frankie. She lied Rose. She's trying to save me from Vinnie's revenge."

"Don't listen to him, mom. His ego is hurt. He's a bum. I'm out of here. I got a good singing voice and I've been offered a job already which I'm taking."

Rose asks who gave her the job.

"Jimmy Pecan, that's who, at The Blue Moon. See ya. Good-bye Frankie."

Rose pipes up again. "That's an awful nice thing you're doing for Frankie." But Carmella is out of the room.

LaVerne and Sam Zocco

I'm dead to the world on the floor, Frankie is sitting dejected, the room is as silent as the grave.

All of a sudden Ricco says, "I think I'm going to faint."

And keels right over.

The next day real trouble comes looking for me at the Club. Sammy Six Toes comes running in. I'm still in a daze about how things worked out with Frankie and Carmella. Frankie is leaving and my pure daughter has emptied her room, taken the Lexus and cashed out her bank account.

"Hey Vinnie," Six Toes says, "there's a whole army outside. This guy is dressed like a general sitting on a white horse."

"Who cares. You follow Carmella like I told you?"

"Sure, boss. She made a beeline right to The Blue Moon. I seen them put her picture outside as their new star attraction."

"Pecan, Pecan. I got to do something about him."

"You want me to call in Brutto Demenza?"

"No, this ain't big enough for him."

"Don't worry about Jimmy Pecan. Right now he's got a lot of men around him. Don't worry we'll get him sooner or later."

The Friggin' Altos
A Crime Family Gone Crazy

"I know. I'm just worried he'll get my pure Carmella first. Hey, you in the blue sash, get that friggin' horse out of my club."

Meanwhile, Frankie is slinking away. He comes into Rose's room to say good-bye."

"Rose, I just came to say good-bye."

"Frankie, Frankie you don't want to leave. Vinnie needs you to stay close to him. Vinnie loves you and I love you. He'll come around."

"Vinnie will never forgive me for making it so he don't trust me anymore. That's what's really hurting Vinnie. And now look what's happened? Carmella's over at The Blue Moon, in the enemy's camp. How are we going to get her back?"

Rose laughs her soft laugh.

"Let Jimmy Pecan have to deal with her for a while. She's so spoiled, he'll be begging us to take her back."

"But, Rose, you heard her. She's wild—she wants danger, and forgive me, wild monkey love."

Rose sighs a long sigh.

"That may be true, but then so did I at her age."

"You Rose, really?"

"You got a lot to learn about women, Frankie."

Jimmy is interviewing Carmella at The Blue Moon. He cannot believe his good luck.

"Carmella, Alto, sitting right here in front of me at The Blue Moon, and on my payroll. What a break—am I a lucky guy or what?"

"You haven't heard me sing, yet. Don't you want me to audition before you make me your star singer?"

"Sure, sure, kid. Go ahead sing something."

Carmella is singing the first line of Blue Moon. She is god-awful.

Jimmy is starting to sweat.

"Enough, enough. That's fine. Hey, Pinky, take Miss Alto to Bertie the bandleader. Tell him to report back to me."

Old Tin Cup Harry, Jimmy's right hand man, lays it on the line.

"Boss, boss, what are you doing? She stunk up the joint. She'll drive all the customers away."

"You're right, Tin Cup. Bertie will know what to do."

Meanwhile, there's many footsteps and sounds of swords rattling at Dante's Inferno. The Generalissimo has found me.

"Senor Alto?"

"Generalissimo."

"It is a fine club you have here. Too bad it will not open."

"Oh? Why won't it open?"

The Friggin' Altos
A Crime Family Gone Crazy

"Because you need a liquor license and I am not about to give you a license."

"Is that so? You always travel with an army with you?"

"Yes, and as you can see they are a wild bunch but under my firm control."

The crowd is yelling and screaming, "Viva, Generalissimo."

Suddenly my waiter, Sergio, comes out to see me.

"What is it Sergio?"

"The cook says he has just seen the Virgin Mary standing on the microwave in the kitchen."

There are shouts, whoops and running feet.

"What happened to your army, General?"

He crosses himself. "Infierno, the Madonna."

I'm beginning to enjoy myself.

"Right now, looks to me like it's a Cuban standoff. I got power—you got power—do you really want a war over a piece of paper?"

"What you say is true, but I own the city. I will shut you out completely. You will have no recourse but to come crawling to me."

I lit up a big cigar and didn't offer him any.

"You don't seem to understand. This is still America and this is still American soil, and I'm a law abiding citizen."

His face turned a bright red.

"Viva Cuba. Liberte Cuba. I own everything, judges, politicians, The Miami Herald, everything. This is not America—this is North Cuba. The government will have to kill me to get it back."

He really was potsa.

"You ever heard of Waco or Ruby Ridge?"

"You ever heard of burning tires and people laying down in the streets to block traffic?"

"You ever hard of Sicily?"

"You ever heard of Donato Dalrymple?"

"How about Janet Reno?"

"How about Goria Estefan?"

"Now that hurts. Then it's war."

"Si, Senor. It is war."

Okay so my senses were off from what had been happening lately. When the General and his army went away to plan god-knows-what against me, I'm sitting in my office in my locked club.

Then I hear a noise and I look up.

"Who's there? Oh, hi. It's late—everyone has gone home. How come you're still hanging around? To tell you the truth I ain't in the mood tonight."

It was Marilyn I was talking to. She looked different in a trench coat and a slouched hat over her eyes. It might have been the clothes that made me see her in a new light, but I really think it was the gun in her hand.

"Is that what you told Lacy too, Vinnie, that you weren't in the mood? Is that why she died because you left her alone and in trouble."

Hey, I was all confused here.

"What has Lacy Love got to do with you?"

"She was my baby sister, you scum. Every time you touched me I wanted to die. I've been waiting and waiting for my chance to get you alone, Vinnie. Pecan don't move fast enough for me. Your time has come, Vinnie. This is for Lacy."

And just like that the gun goes off with a big explosion and the room fills with the stink of gunpowder. I thought she was kidding, then I slowly start to drop to my knees.

"Oh, God, Marilyn, you killed me." I'm coughing and spurting up blood tasting like metal in my mouth. Finally, mercifully, I black out. But, not before I hear her say, "pardon me for not calling 911. Die you bastard, die."

Fifteen minutes later Little Vinnie is working late in his office at the casino. He hears a sound and realizes that Marilyn is standing there in front of his locked door.

LaVerne and Sam Zocco

"Hey, baby. Come on in. How'd you get in? I thought this door was locked. I was just cleaning out my desk. Dickie Blue's taking over. Everyone's gone home. Come over here so I can feel you close."

It took him all that time to realize she has a gun pointed at him.

"Sorry Little Vinnie, but tonight we say good-bye."

He's all confused and not quite getting it.

"What are you saying? Hey you ain't running out on me are you? Where you coming from so late?"

"I just killed your father and now I'm going to kill you. Say your prayers lover."

Vinnie said it felt like when he saw JFK shot, it was so unreal.

He's still not getting it.

"Hey, you're kidding right? Why would you do such a crazy thing?"

"Your father left my sister Lacy to die alone."

He smiled like an idiot.

"Who?"

"Your father was fooling around with my sister Lacy and got her pregnant. He dumped her in New York at some unwed mother's home and came to Florida. She died in childbirth. He had to pay for her death. Sorry, kid, you're like icing on the cake. One less Alto for the world to worry about, get it now? I'm Sorry. See you both in hell."

Then the gun went off like an Atom bomb in his little office and Vinnie grabs his groin and falls into a black pit.

There must be a lesson here about a father and son who are boffing the same woman, and getting shot by the same woman, but I think it would be hard to find anyone that wouldn't label us sick fools, and probably "sloppy seconds," would get in there some place.

Anyway, I was floating in a chilling ice bath like I remember from New York standing looking into the blackness of the East River. Little Vinnie was trying to put his finger in the hole in his groin, but had to give it up when he couldn't control his fingers anymore. Our souls must have passed each other once they were free from our bodies, cause we were both floating, seeing bright white lights, swooshing through tunnels, but then the lights went out and the darkness slammed down like the lid of a casket.

CHAPTER FIFTEEN

The same morning I'm swimming around in fog from being shot poor Rose is having her bandages removed at the hospital. I wanted to be there, and we planned where I would stand with the light shining in on me, so she could see me first thing she sees the world again. I never made it.

"Rose," Dr. Hauser, says to her, "I'm going to take off the bandages now. At first things may be a little bleary, but you must tell me if you see anything at all. If you don't please don't panic. It may take a few moments for your eyes to adjust."

Rose is pulling on a handkerchief, tearing the corner, like she always does when she's nervous. "Oh, I'm so scared and I'm so alone. Big Vinnie upstairs in intensive care, and Little Vinnie in the room next to him. Carmella at The Blue Moon with Jimmy Pecan. I wanted Vinnie to be the first person I saw again." She starts to cry. Hey, Rose, I'm up here fighting for my life maybe. Suck it up already.

The doctor puts a bit of optimism in his voice. "Here we go. I'm just snipping the bandages now. Now, open your eyes slowly, Rose. Remember we

The Friggin' Altos
A Crime Family Gone Crazy

have the shades drawn so it will look dark to you. Tell me what you see?"

"Everything is so dark—no, no, wait, I can see a figure standing in front of me. Sweet, long suffering Ivan! I can see you Ivan—Oh, thank God, I can see you. You're the only one who came."

That bastard Trotsky takes her in his arms and starts kissing her. "Oh, darling, my darling Rose."

Rose pulls back—the poor kid is so vulnerable. "Ivan, stop, it's not right—the two Vinnies are both in the hospital. Ivan, Ivan—"

"What?"

"Please, kiss me again."

While my wife is being seduced down in the Outpatient department, I'm lifting up out of my fog, only I'm weak cause they got me heavily sedated.

"Where am I? Whose there—is that you Rose? Am I dead?"

And there sits Frankie blubbering all over himself.

"Oh, Vinnie, forgive me. I should have never left you."

"Frankie is that you? How am I?"

LaVerne and Sam Zocco

I kinda steeled myself for the news. I didn't feel too bad, but then they say just before you die you feel great.

"The bullet nicked your lung. You're going to be okay with a few weeks rest. You're going to be good as new and I ain't never leaving your side again. Vinnie please don't send me away."

I give him a punch across the chin. He always had a glass jaw. "Frankie, don't ever leave me ever. Who do you love the most? Me or Carmella?"

"You Daddy Vinnie. Forgive me—I must have been crazy—say you forgive me."

He was cranking the head of my bed up so I could see his worried face. "As long as you don't touch Carmella, I forgive you. Now, I want you to go get her out of Jimmy Pecan's hands before he dishonors her. Hey, why you looking so sad?"

I'm thinking he's got a picture of Jimmy Pecan all over Carmella and he's still got feelings. But, no.

"There's something you should know Vinnie."

It was at that precise moment I fell sound asleep. They had me sedated so heavily I figured I was really hurt bad. When I opened my eyes again it felt like just a few minutes had past.

The Friggin' Altos
A Crime Family Gone Crazy

"You wanted to tell me something, Frankie. Go ahead, but make it quick, I'm very sleepy."

"Jeez, boss, that was yesterday. It's just that Lacy's sister Marilyn shot both you and Little Vinnie. She was doing you both, if you get my drift."

Oh, I got it alright. So the little bitch was spending her time travelling back and forth between my son and me. I wanted to laugh. Had I known, I'd have bought her a pair of roller skates. Hell, I'd have bought us all roller skates.

I wanted to tell Frankie I got his drift but I started to get dreamy. I wasn't really taking it all in yet. The irony hadn't sunk in yet. I was talking hogwash.

"Marilyn, what a dish. She was doing Little Vinnie too—that's a hot one. She shot Little Vinnie—" I knew something about that fact should make me feel anger, but all I wanted to do was suck my thumb and go to sleep. Frankie sat and watched me drift away.

"Looks like your boss fell asleep. So it was someone named Marilyn who shot both if them. That's very interesting."

Frankie was agitated.

"Hey, who are you? How did you get in here?"

LaVerne and Sam Zocco

"I'm homicide detective Buenas Noche—Miami Police Department. I'm assigned to the case just in case Little Vinnie Alto dies. Who are you?"

Frankie's steaming. "Get the hell out of here. The Altos are not going to press any charges—they don't even know anyone named Marilyn. This is family business, Noche, take your badge and beat it."

"Okay. Just trying to help. I'll be around."

Frankie opened the window to let the smell of copper out.

Down the hall and next door to my room, was Little Vinnie's room. There was a nurse standing at the foot of his bed looking very worried. Then she gets startled by a sound.

"Sorry, doctor, I didn't hear you come in."

"It's the crepe soles. How's our patient doing today?"

The nurse starts to sniff and cry.

"Oh, he's in so much pain and he's got a high fever. He's been begging for pain medication every hour. The poor boy must be in so much pain and what a weird thing to happen to him. He's so young."

The doctor puts his arms around the nurse and cops a feel.

The Friggin' Altos
A Crime Family Gone Crazy

"It's okay. I got orders from Trotsky his father's lawyer; the boy is to get pain medication anytime he wants. It isn't every day a bullet gets lodged in the groin right at the top of the urine canal where we can't operate to get at it. He's just going to have to wait until it works its way out naturally."

"You mean when he does number one, the water might push the bullet down his—you know what—and make it come shooting out?"

"Yes, it could be anyplace, anytime. He'll never know when it will happen or where it will happen. It's got to be very painful. Give him anything he wants poor guy."

"Will he still be able to make love?"

"Naw, he could ejaculate and kill somebody. What a humiliation."

Me, I'm still in la-la land. Rose is sitting by the bed and I must sense it, cause I'm muttering, "Rose, Rose, I need you—I need you."

Then I hear her angel voice.

"Vinnie darling, I'm here. Open your eyes. Look at me Vinnie, I can see, I can see."

I'm awake, but dopey.

"You can see, you can see." Then I open my eyes and look straight into those cornflower headlights of Rose's. "Oh God, you can see! The bandages are off!" I'm crying all of a sudden. "But, I wasn't there with you Rose. I should have been there. You were all alone."

Rose ain't giving nothing away.

"It's all right, darling. I was scared at first—it was dark and bleary, then everything was clear. It was a miracle."

I'm wide-awake now. "And here I am flat on my back. You must be so angry at me. I should have sent Trotsky to be with you."

She still ain't giving nothing away.

"I told you I'm fine. Let's not talk about it anymore. It was a nightmare, and now it's over. Let's talk about how this happened to you. No one would tell me exactly who shot you or why? I met a Detective Noche in the hall but I couldn't tell him anything."

"That's good Rose, cause you're going to laugh when I tell you what happened."

I ask her to crank my bed up cause I'm feeling wide-awake now. The lung is burning to beat the band but I don't tell Rose that. She comes back to sit by me and I take her hand.

"See, it was an attempted robbery, Rose. Yeah, that's it, an attempted robbery. I was at the office late. It was a complete surprise. I couldn't see who it was. All I know I looked up and the gun went off. And that's all I know."

I think I got her snowed pretty good.

"No, it wasn't a robbery, Vinnie. There's something you don't know yet."

I'm getting suspicious that I ain't as smart as I thought.

"The same person shot Little Vinnie a half hour later. Our son is in the room next door. He hasn't actually come out of his coma yet."

Now I'm distressed and I can't hardly believe it. It's too much for a man to take in so short a time, his wife almost blinded, his son shot. "Little Vinnie was shot too? You left me sleeping here when my son is hurt. How bad is he hurt?"

My delicate Rose leans over and whispers in my ear. "Yeah, the bullet went in there and it's sitting where? Oh, my God. If he pees, what's going to happen? You're kidding."

Delicate Rose shakes her head. "It's true Vinnie. He's in a lot of pain and he has a high fever that's keeping him in a coma. Oh Vinnie, if you know who did this you have to tell Detective Noche and press charges."

I was still thinking about Little Vinnie's wound. "That means if he stands in front of someone and he gets the urge, he could kill someone. What a revolting development this is."

Then I put my mind on what Rose had just said.

"No police. I'll find out myself, and when I do I'll personally take care of them."

Innocent Rose looks at me with those blue peepers.

"Her. It was a woman—she left a long blond hair on your desk and on the gun when she shot Little Vinnie. The gun was untraceable and no fingerprints. She's a mystery woman."

For some reason I was thinking of the rat Pecan.

But I said out loud, "Yeah, a mystery woman."

CHAPTER SIXTEEN

The last we left Carmella she was over with Jimmy Pecan. I didn't know it then but I had driven my little girl away in order for her to protect Frankie from my obsessive ravings. If I had known, it would have made me cry to think I had been the cause of my daughter leaving home. My little girl was growing up right before my eyes. If I had any sense at all I would have known that I could trust her instincts to do the right thing, and that she had the Alto smarts to turn things to her advantage.

After she stunk up The Blue Moon singing, Jimmy Pecan called in Bert his bandleader.

"Okay, Bert. Carmella Alto can't sing worth merda, but she's Vinnie Alto's daughter and I want her to stick around. I want her to be my big new star so what can you do about her?"

Bert had dealt with big shots that wanted a tasty morsel now and again. He had an answer for everything. However, he knew his customers so well he definitely knew what would work and what wouldn't. He sat scratching his head for ten minutes when his eyes lit up with an idea.

"Look, Jimmy, that's easy. We darken the room, put a baby blue spotlight over her head, dress her in a see-through outfit and let her talk her way through the lyrics in a sexy voice. I'll work with her. We'll give her an exotic name like Falfalla, the Italian Butterfly and every guy's tongue in the joint will be hanging out for her."

"What do you think, Tin Cup?"

"Don't ask me, I'm gay."

Pecan allowed himself a small smile.

"By the way Tin Cup, Dickie Blue, from my old gang in Jersey has joined our gang. He's gay too."

Tin Cup perked up at that. "I say Falfalla, the Italian Butterfly, isn't the only one who'll be flitting around."

"Okay," Jimmy says, "do your magic Bert. I want her kept pure and virginal, Capice? And you Tin Cup, I'm holding you responsible to see that she stays that way."

"No problem here, boss."

Suddenly I feel these big gooshy lips kissing me all over my face.

"Vinnie, my son, how are you feeling?"

It was my mother Frances. "Ma. I didn't hear you come in. Just a nick, Ma, I was lucky. Hey, who we got here?"

The Friggin' Altos
A Crime Family Gone Crazy

"Oh, Vinnie, I want you to meet a nice gentleman I met at the condo swimming pool the other day. His names Regis Berkowitz. Isn't he tall, dark and handsome? We've been having a good time going out. He's a widower. Say hello to my son, Regis."

The guy oozed oil from his head to his foot. Even his tongue had a coating of grease from all the snake oil he was passing out.

"Your mother told me about your troubles—I hope we're not disturbing you. Your mother is so lovely and so much fun."

Lovely? Fun? My mother?

I give the guy a shake of the hand and wiped my hand on the sheet.

"Where you from, Regis?"

"Cincinnati."

"Excuse me, could I ask a favor of you. Could you fill up that glass with water and put it here on my bedside table?"

"But, of course."

"While Regis is getting the water, are you going next door to see Little Vinnie? These screws won't let me out of bed to go see him."

"We're going right now."

"Tell him I love him if he's awake."

"Here you are Mr. Alto. A pleasure to meet you."

"Yeah, yeah." The guy was so devious he never cast a shadow.

Then my mother is visiting Little Vinnie in the next room.

"Little Vinnie, how are you feeling?"

She was sitting close to the bed and running her fingers through his thick wavy hair.

"Grandma. Can you ring for the nurse? I need some pain medication. They say my fever's down, but I'm on fire down below."

"Of course, darling. Anything you want you're going to get. Oh, by the way, this is Regis, my new friend. Regis, this is my grandson, Little Vinnie."

Little Vinnie sounded so pathetic and urgent.

"Please, grandma, get some pills. Go down to the nurses station—please."

"My treat, darling. You and Regis talk, I'll be right back."

And off she goes tripping down to the nurse's station. In the meantime slimy Regis is sitting next to the bed his nervous eyes taking everything in.

"So Little Vinnie, that's a very nice grandmother you have. We are like soul mates from the moment we met. I guess even having a lot of money doesn't stop her from being lonely."

"Grandma? Yeah, she's loaded, but her turban's not on too tight, if you know what I mean. She thinks no one loves her because she's old."

"We'll I'm here to fix that."

Then grandma comes back.

"Here you are dear. Tomorrow I'll bring you a whole bunch of pills from home. Do you really think you should be taking four at a time?"

Regis ain't too helpful.

"Leave the boy alone, Frances. He's hurting."

Frankie is down at The Blue Moon. He walks in like he owns the place. It's eerie in the afternoon when there aren't too many customers in the place. But, it was a good time for Frankie to pay the visit. Who comes sashaying out to greet him is Tin Cup.

"Listen, Tin Cup, you got to let me in to see Carmella. You owe me from New York. Remember?"

Tin Cup is feeling relaxed cause Pecan ain't around. The guy is a straight shooter with Frankie cause at one time they were friends.

"Yeah, Frankie, if it wasn't for you I'd be in the slammer with Pecan's old gang doing life. You didn't have to warn me about the raid. I remember, kid. She's in her dressing room down the end of the hall over there. Only she calls herself Falfalla, now. Hey, no patty cake, you know. I'm keeping her innocent for Pecan. Get me?"

"Yeah, yeah. Thanks Tin Cup."

Frankie don't know why his mouth is so dry as he covers the distance to the hall and her dressing room. He only knows he's got to keep it all business with her even though his heart is pounding against his chest.

He taps softly at her door. It opens. She's standing there like a real butterfly. She's all in see through blue with her dark hair piled on her head with silver glittery butterflies holding the curls in place. She seems genuinely glad to see him. Like she's been waiting for him to arrive.

"Carmella, your father sent me. He wants you to come home with me. He says he's sorry about what happened at the house. See he didn't cut me. Everything's Jake. You can't stay here with Pecan."

The last is a painful plea for her to understand.

"Come in Frankie. Sit down. Excuse me while I finish getting ready for my set. The club will be full in about an hour. It's part of my job to mingle."

The Friggin' Altos
A Crime Family Gone Crazy

Frankie is puzzled by her.

"What's the matter with your voice? You sound older—and you look older. What's happened to you, Carmella?"

"I'm Falfalla, now. It means Italian Butterfly. The caterpillar has changed. Am I beautiful, Frankie?" She gets up and parades back and forth in front of him. "Who do you love more? Vinnie or Falfalla. Ow! You're hurting me."

Frankie had grabbed her by the arm. He was angry but he didn't know why he was so angry.

"Listen to me, Falfalla. I want you so much I can taste it. But you're never going to have me—got it? I'd make you cry for mercy—but you're never going to know how it feels. You know why? Because you don't love anyone. You don't know what it means to be grateful or humble. If this is what you really want—to break your mother and father's heart, and be with a psycho like Pecan, then that's it. You deserve each other."

He goes storming out of the room but he don't go home. He heads right for the bar and plops down ordering up strong drinks. The funny thing is, Frankie never drinks. Falfalla watches him go down the hall with this little smile on her mouth. She's my daughter all right.

Back at the hospital I'm talking to Ricco.

"Ricco, I want you to do me a favor. I want you to wrap that water glass there and take it to a lab to have the prints lifted. I want you to check up on those fingerprints and get a history on this guy, Regis Berkowitz."

"Who we talking about?"

"My mom's new boyfriend. He gave me the creeps. Like I said he said his name is Regis Berkowitz, but I think he's lying. I want him checked out all over the country."

"Right. You're looking good today, boss. Aces all the way."

The boob ain't never been shot in the lung.

"Yeah, I get to see Little Vinnie this afternoon. They're letting me use a wheel chair. How's he doing?"

"He's awake and alert. Sitting up in bed."

"Yeah, so what's wrong." Ricco had a face that could never hide anything when he was feeling emotional.

"Well, I don't know much about medicine, but he seems to be taking an awful lot of pain pills. It's like he's flipping down tic-tacs twenty four hours a day a handful at a time."

I wasn't too worried. "Remember, he's got a bullet in a very strange place. I'll check it out myself when I see him."

The Friggin' Altos
A Crime Family Gone Crazy

"A very strange place. I cringe when I think about it." He grabbed his Willy for emphasis.

Later that afternoon, I'm talking to Six Toes.

"Six Toes, get Trotsky in here. He's out in the hall with Rose."

"Sure thing, boss. I guess you heard about Dickie Blue being gay and going over to Pecan. I hear he and Tin Cup got a thing going."

"Yeah, I heard. Hey, never mind here's Trotsky now."

He comes in all suave, polished and flushed.

"You need me Vinne? I was just in to see Little Vinnie with Rose. I don't know how she's managing to stay so strong all the time. Be careful, Vinnie, one of these days she's going to snap."

I ain't on to him yet, but I was feeling the stirrings of a little jealousy for him being near my Rose even for a few minutes. That just wasn't like me.

"Rose? Naw, she's a brick. Now listen I want to talk to you about a couple of things. You know this lawyer kid, friend of Little Vinnie's?"

"Crayton Hooks? Yeah, nice kid and smart."

"I want you to hire him to find Marilyn—our mystery lady who shot me and Little Vinnie. She's Lacy's sister. No one knows Crayton—he'll be able to snoop around. Tell him to go out to see Princess Snow Feather and then Dickie Blue. Pay him big bucks. I want her found before the police find her. This is family business. I want her put on ice until I can talk to her."

"It may be like looking for a needle in a haystack. All the doors may be closed."

I laughed. "You know the Alto philosophy. Never give up and never give in. When you think a door is closed to you, punch a hole through it."

He only grunted.

"The next thing I want to know is what do you know about Walt Disney?"

He's taken back with surprise like I threw ice water in his face.

"Disney? You mean Disney World Disney?"

"Yeah, is there another one? What do you know about him dying?"

Trotsky rubs his smooth chin.

"What everyone else knows, I guess. After he died they froze him. It's what they call, "Cryogenics." The theory is whatever you die of, down the line they will come up with a cure. They keep your body preserved by freezing it, and when they have the cure they thaw you out and re-animate you."

"So it was all about animation for Walt. What a guy! You think they could do that if your heart suddenly exploded that might damage blood vessels, arteries, like that?"

He's looking at me very closely.

"Theoretically, it could be done if they learn how to reconnect nerves, muscles and vessels. They can replace the lost tissue with skin grafts. They do that already. They can also replace a human heart right now. Yeah, I can see, five or ten years down the line, they might be able to do all the rest."

"I want you to get me some brochures from the place they got Disney. I want to read up on it."

"Is this curiosity or do you have something in mind?"

"Just do it. Now, last thing. Now this thing with the Generalissimo. It's war. We got to figure how I can get a liquor license without his approval. And it has to be done legally."

"Well, he could be impeached from office. If you could swing enough votes you could put your own man in there. You could break into the License Department and steal a blank license and fill it in. You could whack him but it would start a helluva investigation with the feds and everyone. Or we could pay him off if he's willing."

"You got to keep in mind this guy is potsa. He's got the whole community behind him. We'd never get enough votes to impeach him even if we trucked in thousands of people to vote, so that's out. If we break into the license department, we still need the seal of the city on it, and that's got to be hidden away like Fort Knox. So that's out. We could whack him but the feds would be down on all the crime bosses in a hurry. The people would go crazy. Too messy. And, there ain't no way this guy is going to take a bribe. It would mean he was weak. There is nothing that means more to this guy than his macho image and his Cuban heritage and being in South Florida. I got it we'll kidnap him! If he's gone long enough they'll have an election and we'll put Crayton Hooks in. He'll get the white vote, the black vote and with the crime bosses help, he'll get the Haitian vote, the Cuban vote and the Italian vote. That's all of South Florida. Yeah, that's what we'll do then. We'll kidnap him and give him a special punishment for being so dense." I felt a whole lot better.

"All this for a liquor license?"

"It may have started that way, but now it's honor."

The Friggin' Altos
A Crime Family Gone Crazy

CHAPTER SEVENTEEN

You'd think I was getting out of jail. That's how happy I was to get out of bed and go and visit Little Vinnie in the wheel chair. I wheel into the room. It's all sunny and bright like a nursery painted yellow. The blinds on the windows are up and you can see the Bay glittering blue and white like diamonds.

It's quiet as a tomb. I position myself by the bed and look into my son's sleeping face. There's dark blue circles under his eyes and his long lashes are twitching from whatever dreams he's having. I try not to let myself think that I almost lost him to the one enemy I couldn't fight: death. He's got a handsome face, I think. Fine and delicate, nothing like mine. He reminds me of a fair Frank Sinatra in his younger days before the ring-a-ding-ding and Dino.

I sit for a while letting him sleep. He seems to be in a real deep sleep, like he was really dead. Then I think about what Ricco was saying about the pain pills, and I start wondering myself if the kid ain't going a little overboard on the stuff. Then I think, hey, he's got a bullet, you know where, how would you be dealing with the psychological fear that situation would cause? Not knowing when it was coming out, not knowing if you'd ever be virile again, not knowing how much pain it would cause when it did finally make an exit down the canal in his Willy. I think I'd want to be knocked out just not to deal with all the questions. Little Vinnie was always an anxious type kid anyway. If there was nothing to worry about, he'd find something. But, I wasn't blinded altogether. If he took enough of those little white pills, he'd get hooked. If he combined it with alcohol, well it could get out of hand. Then he started to stir in the bed and my attention flew to his face.

"Look, Little Vinne, they finally let me come and see you. My boy, are you all right?"

His eyes fluttered open.

"Hand me the glass of water I got to take a pill."

"You better go easy on those. Your speech is slurry, and you look all doped up."

"Poppa, please don't preach. Just get me the water. I'm trying not to think of where that bullet is. It could come shooting out anytime. I could kill someone if they're standing in front of me.

"And the humiliation of getting my father's leftovers. Just because you dumped Marilyn's sister and she died in childbirth. If Ma knew about this, it would kill her. Look at me, this is all your fault."

"Listen Vin, be fair. I didn't know Marilyn was setting me up for a kill. I didn't know she was Lacy's sister. And I certainly didn't know she was leaving me and going to you. If I had, you think I would have let it go on? Look, I'm doing everything to find her before the police do. I'm not pressing charges and neither are you. This is family business. And don't you go talking to the police."

He seemed more settled after that. He even smiled a little.

"There was a detective in to see me named Noche, but I pretended I was sleeping."

I patted his hand. "That's my boy. I got Trotsky and Crayton Hooks looking for her. When we find her you can decide what you want to do with her."

He genuinely laughed. "Crayton my man. When do we get out of here?"

"Just hang in there. Next week. We'll be a happy family again."

Then he kinda passed out. Hell, let him have all the pills he wants. When we get him home I'll put a stop to it. At least that was what I was thinking.

Meanwhile at the Miccosukee Casino, Charlie Coffee is talking to Princess Snow Feather.

"Princess, there's a guy wanting to talk to you. Says his name is Crayton Hooks."

"Does he want a job?"

"No. Just says he needs to talk to you about Big Moccasins."

That gets her attention. "Well, show him in."

In walks Crayton, sharped up to the nines, but elegant. The Princess ain't missing one detail.

"Mr. Hooks, I'm Princess Snow Feather."

He lays it right on the line. "I'm a friend of Little Vinnie Alto. Just a friendly call to give you a message from Big Vinnie. He seems to think someone on the inside gave Marilyn the key to his locked office on the night he was shot. He thinks that was you and that you got the key from Dickie Blue who was still working at Vinnie's club at the time. He also thinks that Dickie Blue gave Marilyn the key to Little Vinnie's locked office on that same night because he was still working here, and got the key from your office, before he went over to Pecan. He further thinks you and Pecan are joining forces to get rid of all the crime bosses.

The Friggin' Altos
A Crime Family Gone Crazy

"Big Vinnie realizes you hate his guts for muscling in on your territory when you want it all for yourself. He can afford to be generous with you instead of satisfying family honor by sending you to the happy hunting grounds. He's more interested in finding Marilyn Love. If you and Dickie Blue produce her, he will forgive your indiscretions. If you don't," he shrugs his shoulders, "it could go hard with your father. As for Dickie Blue, there is always Tin Cup to pay to make amends for Dickie Blue's bad judgment. In addition, you have to give up your dreams of ruling South Florida, and you have to break it off with Jimmy Pecan."

He sees the surrender on the Princess's face.

"Actually, he's doing you a favor cause down the line he's going to take care of Pecan. If you're smart you'll listen. If not there will be a funeral in your teepee very soon, and a big send off for Tin Cup. If I were you I'd talk it over with Dickie Blue, only don't take too long."

He started to walk away then turned around.

"Oh, by the way, you may be thinking a lawyer like me shouldn't be involved, but Little Vinnie is my friend."

She smiled then.

"No, I wasn't thinking that. I was thinking what nice buns you have. Okay, I get the message loud and clear. Maybe you don't know it, but I'm in love with Little Vinnie too. I didn't know Dickie Blue was taking the key to his office to give to Marilyn. I want him for my new Tiger Jim. Just promise me nothing will happen to Marilyn. Friend to friend."

Now Crayton was smiling.

"Damn, that Little Vinnie falls into all the luck. Friend to friend, Marilyn Love will not be harmed."

"Okay, I'll see what I can do."

Trotsky is bringing Rose home from the hospital. Rose is all teary and shook up at the sight of her son doped up and suffering.

"Ivan, I appreciate you bringing me home, but you've got to go now."

Ivan is connivin'.

"How much longer are you going to stay with Vinnie? First you're almost blinded, then Vinnie and Little Vinnie are almost killed. Carmella is working for a real psycho, and there's a war brewing between Vinnie and the Generalissimo. Rose, please, let me take you away. I'll buy an island in the Caribbean—just you and me—I'm the one who loves you, Rose."

The Friggin' Altos
A Crime Family Gone Crazy

Rose is in no mood for arguing.

"Please, Ivan, stop. You think I don't know what Vinnie is and what he does? I took him for better or worse. As long as I know he loves me with all his heart, I can't go with you. Now kiss me for the last time and never speak of this again."

"All right, I'm going. But if you ever change your mind, I'll be around."

Weeks later Rose and I are in bed at the Mansion. Unlike Little Vinnie I ain't lost any of my potency in the sex department. We're bouncing and romping, having a good old time.

"Vinnie, my love," Rose cries breathlessly, "you're still my wonderful lover."

I'm hysterical with expended energy.

"Oh, Rose, it's good to make love to you again when you can see and I can breathe."

"Did you really forgive Frankie and send him to rescue Carmella?" She falls back against the pillows and tries to recover until the next round.

"Yeah, he's the old Frankie. He's vowed to me he's over his love for her—he loves me like old times. He must have been crazy—overcome with sexual madness."

"You mean like when you met me?"

"Yeah. Hey wait—you think—"

Rose is always right on the money.

"I think he wants her more than ever. His love and loyalty to you is what is driving him crazy. What are you doing to our poor boy? What would you have done if my father's demand for loyalty stood between us, Vinnie?"

"I would have kidnapped you. Okay, I'll have a talk with Frankie. So long as he don't touch Carmella, I'll think it all over. Now, come here."

"You're an animal, Vinnie."

Then another voice chimes in. "This is Al. Just letting you know I'm still around. Could you move over just a bit."

Crayton Hooks is in the process of driving Little Vinnie home. Crayton is looking over at his friend and he sees how wasted Little Vinnie really is. A worried look crosses his face and he tries to brighten up the atmosphere with some good-humored teasing that ain't going nowhere.

"Come on, Little Vinnie, Trotsky ask me to bring you home from the hospital. Can you stay awake long enough to tell me what your father is going to do when he finds Marilyn?"

Vinnie is uncoordinated and his arms are flapping around.

"Hand me that bottle of water, I got a pill to take."

The Friggin' Altos
A Crime Family Gone Crazy

Crayton's jaw is getting all tight, his handsome head shaking back and forth.

"Man, you know what you're doing to yourself? First it was pain pills, then it was amphetamines, and now its booze. That's not water that's straight gin. I don't know where the hell you got it in the hospital. You want to kill yourself?"

Vinnie's drunk as a skunk grabbing onto Crayton's shoulder making the car swerve.

"No preaching, okay? I got a bullet in my groin at the opening to my pee canal, and I shared a broad with my father. I'm entitled to stay stoned and smashed forever. If you don't like it, cut yourself loose. Otherwise shut up."

Crayton is trying to stay as cool as he can. He knows it's the booze and the pills talking, but it's hard for any man to see his friend going down the pipe.

"If you want my advice you'll confront your father about your feelings of guilt and shame. Or maybe you think your father showed her a better time."

Vinnie turns on him like a rattler. "Shut up," he spits.

Crayton thinks pushing him will break him.

"Or maybe you really are in love with her. Maybe you don't know the Princess is madly in love with you. Maybe you're the same big baby you've always been. Look at you, going nowhere, doing nothing. Sure blame it on the bullet, or your father, or poor Marilyn. But for heavens sake don't blame it on yourself."

Vinnie throws himself all the way across the seat to grab Crayton. The poor guy has to stop the car or have an accident.

"Get out," Vinnie screams at his friend, "I'll drive myself home."

Crayton tells me he thinks it was worth it to have to walk all the way home to get his friend to start thinking about what he's doing. One helluva guy, Crayton.

The next day Ricco comes into my den. His face tells me all I want to know, but I give him the chance to tell me.

"Boss, I had the fingerprints on that glass analyzed like you told me."

"Good. What'd you find out?"

"This Regis guy's real name is Louie, the groom, Siegel. That's right boss, he's got a rap sheet as long as your arm. He was arrested on ten counts of bigamy, and his last two brides both died mysteriously of food poisoning. You want me to get Brutto Demenza in on this?"

"Naw, we only use him for big jobs. We got to act fast. Get Pete and Santo ready to pay him a visit."

The phone rings on my desk.

I answer the phone, I listen in horror. "Ricco, get the car out. That was the hospital. My mother was just brought in by Louie, the groom. She ate something that didn't agree with her. Like I said get Pete and Santo on the job quick. I'll write down instructions about who and where when I get back. And also tell them I want them to get ready to snatch the Generalissimo when I give them the word. Now, let's go see my mother."

CHAPTER EIGHTEEN

The day my life all fell apart happened a month after I came home from the hospital. I was off doing something important when the front door bell rang at the mansion. Rose always insisted on answering the door herself. She had been in the kitchen supervising our dinner with Dolly the cook. Rose knew our maid, Martha, was upstairs working in one of the bathrooms, so Rose took her apron off and went to the door.

She opens the large door that leads to the huge entrance hall with the spiral staircase that goes upstairs. An unfamiliar face greets her.

"Mrs. Alto. You don't know me, but I have something very important to talk to you about. Could I come in for a few minutes? I promise, I won't take up much of your time."

Holy merda, its Marilyn.

Rose, my sweet unsuspecting Rose, is all hospitality. She was as naïve as Snow White dealing with the witch with the poisoned apple.

"Why, of course dear, please come into the living room. May I get you something—coffee, tea?"

Rose's perplexed by this beautiful young lady with the gorgeous figure and the winning smile. How would you feel if you open the door and there stood Marilyn Monroe? Be honest, you'd be awestruck. Well that's the kind of affect Marilyn had on people, and not just men.

"No thank you," she says. You have to give her credit she didn't even know if I was home or not. She was just going to come in and drop the bomb and leave.

Rose leads the lady of mystery into our beautiful living room, all decorated in gold tones and green accents. She leads her right over to the sofa. "Here we are. Please have a seat. Now, what is this important information you must talk to me about?"

"Did you ever know a girl named Lacy Love?"

There its out and the question hangs in the air because there's a lot more coming. My poor betrayed Rose. Right now Rose perks up at the name.

"Oh yes. Father Gandolfo mentioned her when he bought our house in New York. She was the first client I remember. How did she do? She must have had her baby by now."

"She was my sister, Mrs. Alto. I'm Marilyn Love. Yes, I'm the one that shot your husband and your son, but first please hear what I have to say."

Rose, instead of letting hate enter her heart when confronted by the person that put bullets into me and Little Vinnie, looks at the poor girl's face and sees the pain and agony in her eyes. I told you Rose had a big heart along with a lot of brains.

"All right, Marilyn. I'm willing to listen to anything you have to say. But, don't mind if I do it with a mother's aching heart, and a very suspicious mind."

And that's when Marilyn poured out the whole story to Rose.

The minute Marilyn leaves, Rose is on the phone to Ivan.

"Ivan, I've just had a visit from Marilyn Love, Lacy Love's sister. She told me all about Vinnie's affair with that girl, and why she shot Vinnie and Little Vinnie. I'm trying not to cry but my whole world is shattered. I want to leave Vinnie. I can't be happy with a man who lies and deceives me, running around with other women, sharing his intimate love with anything in skirts. Yes, I know I sound numb. I guess I'm in shock, but I'm alert enough to know what I want to do. I can't stay here one more minute. Will you come and get me,

Ivan. Please, Ivan, take me away like you promised to that deserted island. Do you still want me?"

You know and I know she didn't have to ask twice.

"Oh, Rose, do I still want you? This is a dream come true, my darling. Stay right where you are. I'll be right over to get you."

"I'll be waiting." She puts down the phone and stares at it for a long time.

"Rose?"

She jumps in fear because the voice has called her back from her memories.

"Oh, Al, you scared me. I suppose you heard. Don't try and talk me out of it."

"I wouldn't think of it Rose. I'll explain it all to Vinnie when he comes home tonight. I think a few days away would do you a world of good, just don't go thinking it's the end of the world."

"Thank you, Al. I couldn't stand talking to him or even sitting down and writing a note. I can never forgive him, Al."

"Never is a long time, Rose. I should know."

The second catastrophe came right on the heels of Marilyn's visit. Ricco has gotten some bad news and he tried to figure out what the right thing would be to do about it. He don't find Rose home, and I'm not there, so he calls Crayton Hooks.

"Crayton, we haven't talked but I'm Ricco—Vinnie Alto's friend. I just got a call from the police about Little Vinnie. I got my hands full right now and I can't find Ivan Trotsky anywhere. I know you're Little Vinnie's friend—"

Crayton is stiffening for the news that Little Vinnie is dead.

"Ricco, what is it? I was with Little Vinnie this afternoon but he was high on drugs and alcohol and he threw me out of the car."

"Well, see, that's it. It seems he somehow was driving the wrong way on I-95 and he smashed into an oncoming car."

Crayton grabs his head and plops in a chair.

"Oh, God. Was he hurt? Is he dead?"

He's so afraid it's going to be death.

"Well, that's what's so strange. According to witnesses, Little Vinnie and the driver of the other car left their cars in the middle of the road and walked off singing at the top of their lungs. The driver of the other car told one of the witnesses Little Vinnie needed help and he was taking him to his home to straighten Little Vinnie out."

Crayton blows out a long breath of relief.

The Friggin' Altos
A Crime Family Gone Crazy

"Did anybody get the guy's name or where he was taking Little Vinnie?"

Ricco laughs. "You ain't going to believe this, but all the witnesses say it was Jimmy Buffet and he was taking Little Vinnie to the Keys to sober him up cold turkey."

Crayton laughed out loud.

"If that's true I think it's the most wonderful thing that could happen to Little Vinnie. Don't worry about the police I'll take care of it."

"Thanks. You're okay. I think Little Vinnie is lucky to have you for a friend."

"And I think Big Vinnie is lucky to have you for a shooter."

Ain't that a bunch of crap.

Let's see, while all this is going on, Frankie is at The Blue Moon for the thirtieth night in a row. He's been sopping up Rum and Coke until his eyes are pointing in two different directions, and he's a sloppy drunk. Jeez, how I hate sloppy drunks. The bartender feels the same way I do.

"Hey fella. Don't you think you've had enough? You've been sitting there all evening and we're getting near closing time. Every time Falfalla comes out and sings you start crying. I haven't called Mr. Pecan yet, but if you don't leave peaceful like, we'll have to get rough."

LaVerne and Sam Zocco

Frankie can barely lift his head and his words are slurring all over the place.

"Just you go ahead, get Pecan out here. Drunk or sober, I'd be happy to take on that psycho."

Suddenly, from out of nowhere there's Falfalla, oops, Carmella standing by Frankie's side.

"What's going on here, Joe?" All bartenders are named Joe.

"Oh, hi. It's this creep here—he's smashed and looking to make trouble. Can you do something with him. Do you know this guy?"

"It's okay," she smiles. "I know him. Call a cab, I'll make sure he leaves without any trouble. Come on Frankie, let me help you off the stool. Put your arms around my neck. That's it, now just lean on me."

"Hey, where's Pecan. Somebody goin' get Pecan?"

"Come on Frankie. Not tonight, Mr. Pecan has gone home. Now, we're going to my place so you can sleep it off."

"We going to your place. Who are you?"

"Does it matter?"

"No, you're right. Let's go to your place."

And she pours him out of there.

That night I come tooling home like everything is peaches. No sooner I walk in the door I can sense something's not just kosher. Don't ask what it was, but married people are so in tune that when something is going on with one the other one can feel it. It didn't take long for the roof to cave in.

"Rose—Rose—I'm home." What a schnook I was like I thought she'd be excited that I was home.

Then that soft Italian accent fills my ears and I know the worst has happened.

"Sorry Vinnie, she's not here."

I collapse on the sofa that was still hot from Marilyn's ass and I just know she's been in the room.

"Al. What do you mean she's not here? Where is she? She's always here when I get home." I'm starting to tear up already.

Al sits down across from me and looks at me with pity in his eyes. Imagine a ghost from hell feeling pity for me. He ain't enjoying this either. For a guy that used to be so cocky, he's come a long way in the compassion department.

"She had a visitor today. Marilyn Love came to see her. She told her all about your affair with Lacy and how Lacy died. She even told her about shooting you and Little Vinnie. She was overcome with grief and brandy."

LaVerne and Sam Zocco

I jump up, but Al stands in front of me and pushes me back down on the sofa. He can see I'm already out of my mind with worry—distraught the doc would say.

"Prepare yourself, Vinnie. She's run off with Ivan Trotsky. He's been in love with her for a long time. Don't delude yourself that she's vulnerable and he's taking advantage of her. Ivan's been the only one around here that's had real concern for Rose. Where were you Vinnie and what were you thinking? Were you there when the bandages came off and she didn't know if she would ever see again? No, but Ivan was. Did you give the least thought to her when you were bouncing around with Lacy and Marilyn? Did it make you feel the least bit uncomfortable that you were leaving your unborn kid in New York without a backward glance for Lacy or the baby? So, let's talk about your ex-partner Tony Sweets? You didn't really have to order his murder. The books were safe and so was everything else. Your childhood friend, and you whack him like a pesky mosquito when he asked for your understanding and strength. Then there's Frankie and the way you been driving that poor kid mad. Just look into your heart and see how hard you've been riding Little Vinnie. Anyway, if you keep going the way you are my punishment isn't going to seem too bad."

I kept thinking I had heard this speech from that ghost that pops up every Christmas in some Christmas Carol or something.

"I see where you're going with this Al. Just tell me where did Ivan take her?"

Al gives a big sigh and sits back down.

"An isolated island in the Bahamas. She didn't say which one. You have to give her time to think."

My voice sounded so feeble and whiny.

"But she's with Ivan."

"No, she's with your history. If she comes back it won't be anyone's choice but her own. Besides, Ivan loves her and he's a lawyer. He's got several days to make his summation speech. If she turns him down he'll know he gave it his all."

Princess Snow Flower is pacing back and forth at the Casino. She's got Dickie Blue in the office and he ain't looking so good.

"Crayton Hooks was here and he gave me a message from Big Vinnie."

"You mean that new lawyer Trotsky hired, the one with the nice buns?"

"That's him. Big Vinnie knows that you gave me the key for Big Vinnie's office to give to

Marilyn so she could get in and shoot him. He also knows that you took the spare key from the casino here to give to Marilyn so she could get in and shoot Little Vinnie. He knows you been working for Pecan right along, that you're in love with Tin Cup and that I hate Big Vinnie's guts and that I'm in love with Little Vinnie."

"Wait a minute, could you repeat that?"

"What part didn't you understand?"

"Let's see, I took the key from the Inferno to give to you to give to Marilyn—I'm lost."

Snow Feather's eagle feather is drooping.

"Look, never mind. We both did a bad thing and if we don't produce Marilyn for Big Vinnie, he's going to kill Tin Cup and my father. Got that?"

"Yeah, that I got. Poor little Tin Cup, I'm going to miss him."

The eagle feather drops another inch.

"We got no choice. We got to give Vinnie Marilyn Love. The sooner we give her over to him, the better. Where do you have her stashed?"

"She's in a safe place. You know Pecan ain't going to like this. He had dreams of you and him taking over the whole crime business in Miami."

"Listen to me you creep, Vinnie Alto is going to kill Pecan for almost blinding Rose, and for

The Friggin' Altos
A Crime Family Gone Crazy

encouraging Marilyn to hit him and Little Vinnie. You still want to back Pecan?"

"I think I get it now."

"Good. Then pick up Marilyn and deliver her to Crayton Hooks, then finally we'll have paid our debt."

"Once we give her back you're sure we'll be off the hook?"

"Vinnie Alto said, once he had Marilyn we're out of it. We got no choice."

Then Frankie wakes up in Carmella's bed.

He's got the mother of all hangovers and he's looking around stupid like trying to figure out where the hell he is. Then here comes my daughter in a green satin teddy and nothing else. My little girl, my pure sweet Carmella, what can I say. Please You go on with the scene, I can't stand it.

"Jeez, Carmella, how did I end up here in your bed?"

"Don't you remember Frankie? You were drunk as a skunk at The Blue Moon. The bartender was going to throw you out, so I brought you here to sleep it off."

"I appreciate that. Hey, you undressed me. You took me right down to my shorts. Just turn your back and I'll get out of your life. Hey, Hey, what are you doing? You can't crawl in bed with me!"

"Frankie—I love you so much, please don't send me away. For real now, I turned eighteen yesterday. I'm legal!"

"Goddaughter, I just love your face."

"Oh, Frankie. You're lips are so soft. Make me cry for mercy."

"Oh baby. You won't be sorry will you?"

"Never, Frankie, never."

And that's the end of Falfalla and her knobbed antennae.

The Friggin' Altos
A Crime Family Gone Crazy

CHAPTER NINETEEN

Right in the middle of all this upheaval that was going on I get a call from my mother. Now you know she and I made up a while back before we moved to Florida. I had given her my two hours a week, and she had stayed reasonably sane. But when she lugged this Louie, the groom, Siegel into the picture I had to look out for her best interests. Well my version of her best interests were not the same as what she saw as her own best interests. She had no idea her charming Mr. Berkowitz was a ten-time bigamist with a penchant for poisoning his brides for their money.

I had already alerted Pete and Santo, my two torpedoes, that they would soon get the call to put Mr. Berkowitz out of his misery. That's why when I got this call it brought this problem right into the forefront of my mind.

"Hi Vinnie, baby, it's your mother."

"Ma. How do you feel?"

She seemed surprised then she remembered the day she had spent in the hospital being sick all over the front of me. The doc thought it was botulism, but I knew, just looking at Louie, the groom's face, it was some sort of poisoning. After that day I was looking for a way to get some information from her about Louie and this phone call seemed to be sent from heaven, only what she had to say wasn't sent from heaven.

"I'm feeling on top of the world, son. Regis has asked me to elope with him. We were in the lawyer's office to sign a pre-wedding agreement. I told him where all my money and investments were handled, and of course my insurance policy. Tomorrow we're going to be off to Europe."

"Wait, wait, Ma. Why are you eloping? Why not have a nice ceremony with the family here at the house?" Of course I didn't mention that Rose had left me forever.

"We don't want any fuss, Vinnie. Besides, Regis, Mr. Berkowitz thinks you don't like him."

Ah, she had finally given me my opening.

"Listen give me the number of his apartment. I want to go talk to him personally. After all you're my mother, I worry about you."

She laughed with pleasure and pride.

"That's a lovely thought darling. Let's see, Mr. Herkowitz is in 309, Mr. Turkowitz is in 308, and Mr. Berkowitz, Regis is in 307 right next door."

"I'll be there tomorrow morning Ma. We'll have breakfast. Then we can give you and Mr. Herkowitz—I mean, Mr. Turkowitz—sorry Ma,

Mr. Berkotwitz, Regis a nice wedding like I want my mother to have."

"You're a wonderful son, love. See you tomorrow morning."

Well, there wasn't any time to waste. I looked at the notes I had scratched on the pad in front of me. Then I called Ricco in.

"Ricco, get Pete and Santo on the phone. Have them meet you somewhere and give them these instructions. This is very important. This job has to be done tonight. Without fail."

Ricco looked at the note and nodded his head. "Right, boss, without fail."

Well now we're on the deserted island with Rose and Ivan. They have had a long flight over, a long wait while their house was being made ready, and both of them are fairly exhausted. Still, Ivan ain't giving up. I guess this guy ain't been laid since college.

"Rose, darling. You've done nothing but cry all the way here and now you've been sick in the bathroom for the last two hours. I'm beginning to think tonight is not the night for our love."

Rose is apologetic and green around the gills.

"I'm so sorry Ivan. You've been so sweet, bringing me here knowing it would interfere with your business, knowing how expensive it would be, knowing the time it would take for me to heal."

"Knowing Vinnie would shoot me."

"Yes, that's why I feel just awful telling you I cannot stay. I must go back now."

Trotsky is blowing steam through his nostrils and almost crying.

"Go back! But we just got here. I haven't even had a chance to smell the hibiscus. Why on Earth would you want to leave?"

"A week ago when I started getting sick I thought it was the flu. But, I've just taken the test in the bathroom and it's positive."

"Tell me its appendicitis."

"Oh, darling, long suffering Ivan. I must go back because I'm pregnant with Vinnie's and my child. Isn't it wonderful?"

Now he is crying.

"Thrillsville."

There is a knock on Crayton Hook's door. He has fallen asleep in the chair but is immediately awake. He looks at the clock and can't believe the time.

"It's 3 o'clock in the morning—who is it?"

There is a breathless voice from the other side of the door.

"Are you Crayton Hooks?"

The Friggin' Altos
A Crime Family Gone Crazy

"You got that right. Who are you?"

"I'm the murderess you've been looking for. Could you please open the door. Princess Snow Feather and Dickie Blue sent me to you. I'm the one who shot Vinnie and Little Vinnie. I'm ready to give myself up to Vinnie Alto if he don't kill Tin Cup and don't kill Chief Panther Bob."

Crayton gets up and walks over to the door. He opens the door. There is no light in the hallway and he squints his eyes to see Marilyn who is in the shadows.

"I'm a lawyer. I work with Ivan Trotsky, Vinnie's lawyer. We've been looking all over for you. Please, come on in."

"How are Vinnie and Little Vinnie? I want you to know I did it for my sister Lacy. She died of a broken heart and childbirth over that bum Vinnie Alto. I had to do something."

She still hasn't moved to cross the threshold. She seemed fearful and distressed. Crayton tries to make her feel better about me killing her when I get my hands on her. In some ways he was really out of touch with reality. He had seen too many mob movies too.

"Vinnie's fine. Little Vinnie ain't checked in yet. He's off with Jimmy Buffet staying away from pills and booze."

LaVerne and Sam Zocco

Marilyn steps through the door. Her hair is windblown and her eyes are kind of sparkly. She's wearing nothing but a sweater and jeans, no bra.

"What's the matter. Oh, I know, I look terrible. I didn't have a chance to get fixed up. Dickie Blue just came and got me and put me in a cab for this address. You look so strange."

Crayton is thunderstruck like I was, like everybody is that sees her for the first time.

"No, I just got a look at your face in the light. Lord-a-mercy."

My mother calls me screaming and crying.

"Vinnie, Vinnie, oh, God, it's terrible, terrible."

I knew Pete and Santo have done the job.

"Ma, calm down. What's terrible? Are you sick—what's going on?"

She's gushing and coughing and finally she manages to spit it out.

"My Mr. Berkowitz, my Regis is dead. Oh, Vinnie, the police just left. They asked so many questions. They got all three, all three."

I perk up at this news.

"What do you mean they got all three?"

"The police said the killers were definitely looking for Regis but they must have got the names mixed up. First they went to Mr. Herkowitz in 309 and shot him. Then they realized they made

The Friggin' Altos
A Crime Family Gone Crazy

a mistake. They went next door to Mr. Turkowitz in 308 and stabbed him. This time they rifled through his wallet and got out his driver's license to be sure. When they saw he wasn't Regis, they made their way next door to my beloved's apartment and held him against the wall while one of the men phoned down to the gate to make sure it was Regis. Then, oh Vinnie, then they poured poison down his throat and left him for dead. The police said he lived long enough to write a note that said, "Santo Peter, Santo Peter." You wouldn't think a dying Jewish gentleman would be praying to St. Peter would you?"

"Go to bed Ma. I'll talk to you in the morning. Sometimes things turn out for the best. You just got to believe that."

"Thank you Vinnie. I feel much better now."

The first chance I get I ask Ricco if he's heard from Pete and Santo. He says they just called. That they wanted to tell me they never could read my handwriting.

I'm sitting in the chair right after that when the phone rings. It's Ivan the wife-stealer. I'm shocked to hear his voice. Right then I know something is wrong.

"You Russian nut. Where the friggin' hell is Rose? Where's my wife? I thought she was off on some island with you."

"Listen to me Vinnie and don't go crazy. Rose is in the hospital."

"WHAT!!!"

"Now just listen for once in your life. She found out she was pregnant with your baby when we got to the island. She was coming back to you. It was the trip. First to the island and then back again. She lost the baby Vinnie. She's in the hospital but she's delirious. She thinks she had the baby. She's asking for them to bring the baby to her. You got to do something right away Vinnie. I'm afraid if she finds out she lost the baby she'll harm herself."

"I'm on my way. You I'll deal with later."

I'm on my way out the door when I bump into two people who are standing on my doorstep. I don't recognize either one of them.

"I'm sorry I can't stop to talk. Whoever you are, I'm in a big hurry."

Then I see it's a priest and a nun.

"I gave at the office."

"Are you Vinnie Alto from New York."

"Yeah, that's me, but like I said, I'm in a hurry."

The Friggin' Altos
A Crime Family Gone Crazy

These people can't take a hint.

"We've never met but I'm Father Gandolfo. We bought your house and opened a Catholic home for unwed mothers. Lacy Love was my first client. Do you remember Lacy?"

That slows me down a little for just a moment.

"Of course I remember her. She died a while back. What's this got to do with me?"

"Yes, the poor child died, but not before she gave birth to your son. I've come all the way from New York to give you your son if indeed he is your son. I'll just need a blood sample to prove you're the father and the sister here will turn the baby over to you tomorrow. Hey, give that child back to Sister Sludge."

I'm running as fast as I can go with the baby in my arms.

"Sorry. I need my boy right now. I'll see you tomorrow."

And I was out of there.

I arrive at the hospital and come skidding through the front doors. I tell the nurse at the front desk the story and she calls up to the doctor on Rose's case for orders.

"Now, Mr. Alto, the doctor has approved your visit but remember your wife is weak and delirious."

"Don't worry. I won't do anything to upset her. Here nurse hold the baby while I put on this mask and gown."

"But Mr. Alto you can't take that baby in there with you. This is highly irregular."

"The doc said it would be okay. You can call him back and check. He said it when I talked to him while you went to get me this stuff. Okay, now give me the baby and open the door."

The room is dark except for a small light over Rose's head where she's laying in the bed. She ain't looking so hot and she is looking around at things like she's in a trance and don't know where she is. She don't even know me when I sit on the bed.

"Rose, Rose, are you awake? Look what I've got for you Rose. It's your baby—our baby. Rose, open your eyes and look.

"Here Rose, take our new born baby in your arms."

Her voice is frail and low.

"Vinnie, is that you Vinnie."

"Yes Rose."

"See our new baby. They just brought him into me." Her eyes are bright and a little crazy. "Vinnie, our new baby has teeth and just called me mommy."

The Friggin' Altos
A Crime Family Gone Crazy

"Yeah. Well, we'll talk about that later."

CHAPTER TWENTY

The next day Rose was up early playing with the baby, and I excused myself quietly to go home. Ricco had called and told me Crayton Hooks was on his way over and he was bringing Marilyn Love with him. I took one look at the way they were holding hands when they came through the door and realized love had come to the two of them. Well, it was a good thing. My lust for Marilyn had disappeared with a part of my lung, and Crayton was free, black and twenty-one; hopefully he knew what he was doing.

"Thanks Crayton for bringing Marilyn here to see me. You can go wait out in the hall."

Crayton looked like he might argue about that, but Marilyn stepped in, put her fingers across his mouth and smiled. Crayton looked across at me with a worried look.

"You're not going to do anything rash are you Mr. Alto?"

I smiled and patted his shoulder.

"What—like string her up to the chandelier? You been seeing too many mob movies. No, I swear, I just want to talk to her. You can have her in twenty minutes or so. Now, go and stop fretting."

I led Marilyn into the living room and shut the double doors leaving Crayton outside nosing around the downstairs rooms.

When she's settled in on the couch and me in the chair across from her, I appraise our situation.

"So, Marilyn, we meet again."

I can see she's suffering from guilt and remorse. I can understand her wanting to kill me for hurting someone she loved. It's family honor. Of all people in the world I understand that better than anyone. She's got big tears rolling down her cheek and she looks like a lost child.

"I'm truly sorry, Vinnie. I must have been out of my mind with grief for Lacy. You'll always be the one who dumped her and left her to die. Now, I can see killing you would never have taken away the pain of losing her. I'm even more sorry about Little Vinnie. He was a completely innocent bystander. And your wife Rose, well you're a lucky man, Vinnie, she's an angel who loves you very much."

It was my turn to feel small and insignificant in the presence of Rose's spirit in that room. I wondered if what she had told Al were true, that she would never be able to forgive me.

I laughed to lighten the mood.

"Well you'll always be Marilyn the stripper, lover, shooter to me. Take that worried look off your face—I ain't going to snuff you. I have something very important to tell you. Maybe it'll take the hate your feeling for me out of your heart just a little."

She balled her hands up in front of her nervously and looked at me with desperate expectations.

"If you could do that for me, I'd be grateful for the rest of my life."

I pulled my chair closer to the couch.

"Do you know Father Gandolfo, Lacy's priest?"

She looked a little surprised but nodded her head yes.

"Well he was here last night. He came to bring me the baby boy Lacy had before she died." Her eyes flew wide in surprise. I held up my hand to signal her to let me finish.

"He took some blood to make sure the baby was mine." She couldn't contain herself a second longer.

"Lacy had a baby? But no one told me. Oh, my God, I've got an Alto for a nephew! Poor Lacy, she wanted to be a mother so badly." She started blubbering so hard I had to go over and put my arms around her.

"Hold it, hold it. I know how you feel kid, Lacy was an okay broad. But, please let me finish what I want to say."

She seemed to stop sobbing so much and little by little she calmed down to just laying with her head on my shoulder.

"I don't blame you for taking the shot at me—I was wrong to get involved with Lacy and leave her like I did. I should have told Rose and taken my medicine so I could have done right by your sister, but I was scared. Can you understand that?"

She nodded her head yes against my shoulder.

"You're right though about shooting Little Vinnie or making him a part of our affair. I know you wanted to hurt me anyway you could, but making love to a man's son while you're still warm from his father's embraces does nothing for family unity. Anyway, it's up to Little Vinnie to forgive you for that. That's between you and him.

"What I wanted to tell you is that Father Gandolfo brought me the results of the blood test this morning. It turns out the kid ain't mine—it was never mine! Now, doesn't that make you feel better?"

She raised her head off my shoulder and smiled. It's the first time I've ever seen Marilyn smile.

"He had the results of another DNA test. He told me it was from the real father. He also showed me a package, all tied up, that the real father had given Lacy when he first heard she was pregnant. She never opened it."

She was wiping her eyes with her handkerchief.

"Well, who is the real father of Lacy's baby?"

I shook my head.

"The good father wouldn't tell me. But, here's why I wanted to see you. Rose had a miscarriage yesterday. She was delirious thinking she had given birth to our baby. I stole the baby from Father Gandolfo and brought him to Rose. In her confusion she thought he really was our new baby and I didn't have the heart to tell her the truth until she was feeling better. She loves that baby with all her heart. I don't think she'll ever give him up. Since you're Lacy's next of kin I was wondering if you could find it in your heart to leave your nephew with Rose and me. You can come see him anytime you want to. You'll always be his Aunt Marilyn. And you'll be giving Rose a wonderful gift for which I'll always be in your debt. You met Rose. You've seen what kind of woman she is.

The Friggin' Altos
A Crime Family Gone Crazy

She'll adopt you and Crayton right into our family. Say yes, and there will be no more talk of police or charges or anything. But, don't do it for that. Do it because the baby will always be happy and loved."

I could see she was struggling a little, then she's all smiles.

"In a strange way I think Lacy would be very happy with Rose raising her son. I lead such an unpredictable life it's for sure the baby would be better off with Rose. Only, it's got to be for real that I can see him anytime I want to."

I crossed my heart. "Scout's honor."

She gave me a kiss on the cheek and stood up ready to go. I could see all trace of hate had left her completely. When I opened the living room doors she walked straight into Crayton's arms and the two of them went happily out the front door.

Now, all I had to do was face Rose.

I peeked my head around the door to Rose's room and found her sitting up in bed. The light from the afternoon sun was making her blond hair red with its rays. She looked beautiful.

"Rose, how are you feeling? You're not delirious anymore?"

She was kind of distance, detached, mad as hell at me.

LaVerne and Sam Zocco

I came and sat in the chair by the side of the bed.

"No, Vinnie. I'm perfectly fine and my mind is clear and sane again. They just took the baby away. He was sound asleep."

I clear my throat a little and look her straight in the eye.

"Rose, we got to talk. I was unfaithful to you, Rose. I must have been nuts. Having a wonderful loving wife like you, and going out with some babe like Lacy, but sometimes a man is an animal. I never wanted to show you that side of me."

She just sat there and stared. She wasn't making this easy for me.

"I was ashamed to tell you. Then she got pregnant. She told me the baby was mine. We were moving to Florida, so I dumped her for Father Gandolfo to take care of. But, Rose, it turns out the baby wasn't mine but everyone thought it was, even Father Gandolfo. He brought him to me all the way from New York last night. It was like God sent him when you had the miscarriage. I just knew I couldn't let you suffer Rose, so I brought the little tyke to you last night and told you he was our baby. I know how much you love him, darling. I talked to Marilyn Love today Rose. All is forgiven with her. She said we could keep the baby if you want him cause she's the next of kin. Only Father Gandolfo knows who the real father of the baby is and he won't tell me. Anyway, if we adopt Marilyn into our family, she wants you to have Lacy's baby. She thinks Lacy would want it too. Now, it's up to you. Do you want to keep the baby, Rose?"

"I want that baby more than life itself, Vinnie. I've already named him that's how sure I was you were going to be able to get him for me. I named him after your father: Pissimo."

The sweat was pouring off my face.

"Does this mean you forgive me?"

"Yes, Vinnie, I forgive you. But from now on if you want hot monkey sex, you promise to come to me."

"Why, Rose, you surprise me. Even if I want to—"

"Anything."

I laughed out loud.

"This is a great country we live in."

We both laughed at that.

Okay, so that turned out all right. Everyone around me is happy except me. I consider myself a modern man, but when I'm betrayed, the old Sicilian dagger gets me right in my heart, and I can't rest until I get my revenge. You might have thought I should have quit while I was ahead with Marilyn taken care of, Rose happy, and my mother safe. But, no, there are some things you can't back down from and so I found myself forging ahead, driven to gather up my enemies and take care of them all at one time.

I gave Ricco the job of finding the Generalissimo, Ivan Trotsky and Jimmy Pecan, and kidnapping all three. I thought those were all I had to deal with but I soon found out I as wrong.

I told Ricco at the time to snatch them all and bring them to the soundproof cellar of Dante's Inferno. I needed time to decide what to do with them. Each one deserved a fitting punishment for their crimes against me. Ivan for stealing Rose. Pecan for nearly blinding Rose, conniving with Marilyn to kill me, and my son, Little Vinnie, and for shooting me when we were young. The Generalissimo goes without saying, he wouldn't give me the fucking liquor license.

Ricco could see the blood in my eyes and the dark Sicilian look on my face. He figured he was going to need help to do the job. I told him it had to be a surprise and it had to be now.

It was then that I agreed this job was big enough for Brutto.

The Friggin' Altos
A Crime Family Gone Crazy

Ricco had only one comment, "I'd hate to be in their shoes. Okay, boss, consider it done."

The next day my son, Little Vinnie, returned to the mansion. It was Sammy Six Toes that told me. My joy knew no bounds.

"Is he all right, Sammy? Remember he's in a delicate condition with that bullet lodged—you know where. How does he look?"

Sammy settled my fears.

"You know he's been staying with Jimmy Buffet for over a month. You could have gotten him at anytime. How come you left him in the Keys with Jimmy?"

"Latitudes and attitudes, Sammy. I thought Jimmy's layback lifestyle might change Little Vinnie's personality and get him off the pills and booze."

"I think it did the trick, boss. He looked sober and drug free. But, I got to tell you he was wearing a Hawaiian shirt, flip-flops on his feet, and strumming a ukulele. And he had a far-away look in his eyes."

I ran past him and bounded up the stairs.

I called back down to Sammy. "Oh, my God. We may have pushed him too far the other way—he may have become a beach bum."

I stopped in the middle of the hall upstairs and caught my breath. Then, I casually walked into Little Vinnie's bedroom. He was laying on his bed staring up at the ceiling.

"Little Vinnie, my son, I'm so glad you're home. How do you feel?"

He never took his eyes off a little spider he was watching crawling across the ceiling.

"Have you ever lain out in a hammock at night and counted the stars, or climbed a coconut tree and taken a really good look at how the palm leaf is constructed. Music comes across the water and the breeze is like music in your ears." His voice sounded dreamy and far away.

"No, I never have, Little Vinnie. Tell me more."

"Island women with hibiscus in their hair massage you all over with Patchouli oil. They feed you Key Lime Pie and Mango juice, play submarine with you in the bathtub, and in the steamy humid night they come to your room and take turns—"

"I get the picture. Er, Little Vinnie, is that bullet still lodged—you know where?"

"Yes, father, but Jimmy says to everything there is a season. One day the time will be right for that bullet to come shooting out. Until then, why worry."

"Well, until then don't point at anyone."

He got up off the bed and came over to hug me.

"Little Vinnie, could you turn a little towards the window."

Then I get real bad news. Ricco comes running in. He tells me Jimmy Pecan is threatening to run away with Carmella and he's saying Lacy's baby is his and he wants him. What a revolting development this is. Father Gandolfo says he has to be fair and test Jimmy's blood to see if he's any kin to the real father.

"Listen, that priest is all over like merda. We're going to have to kidnap him along with Pecan. When is this all going to happen?"

Ricco turns sad bloodhound eyes on me.

"I think we got to bring in Brutto Demenza. This is going to be a big job."

As much as I get racked with chills I have to agree with Ricco.

"You're right Ricco, I'm sorry to say it, but this is a big enough job for Brutto Demenza. Where is Brutto now?" Ricco is always up on those things.

"It ain't going to be easy to get him."

"Why, what's he doing these days?"

"He's Jesse Ventura's keeper."

"Momma Mia, now that's a big job."

"Boss, you sure you want to go through with this? Ivan, Jimmy Pecan, the Generalissimo, and Father Gandolfo?"

"Silencio! Not only do we kidnap them, it means the Italian ritual of Morte o Peggiore, death or worse."

Ricco's eyes bug out.

"Morte o Peggiore? Those poor bastards."

And then the worse thing that could possibly happen does. Frankie finally comes home.

"Where the hell have you been, Frankie? Poor Ricco and Santo and Pete have had to handle everything around here by themselves. And where's Carmella?"

Frankie dropped to his knees.

"She's with me. She's in the car outside. I love her, Vinnie. I feel just like you did when you spotted Rose for the first time."

"Hey, watch your mouth." But Jimmy don't have Carmella.

"Please, Vinnie, try and understand, she turned eighteen a few days ago. I've been going through hell. You might as well kill me now, Vinnie. Carmella and I have been to Motel 6. I know she's your little daughter but you have Pissimo now.

Please Vinnie, my friend, my boss, my idol, have mercy. Please understand."

"You have dishonored my little girl. You have broken your promise to me. You are a traitor and a liar."

I ran out into the hall to find Ricco.

"Take this traitor right now down to the cellar at Dante's Inferno. Tie him up good. He has touched my daughter. He is no better than Jimmy Pecan or Ivan Trotsky."

"He dies. Morte o Peggiore. When you have captured them all and they are all down at the Inferno, call me, and then we will call Brutto Demenza to come into town and whack the losers."

Ricco was practically crying as he took hapless Frankie by the arm and led him away.

"Hey, Ricco." My right-hand-man turned with a smile thinking I had changed my mind about Frankie.

"Tell Brutto, coach, no first class."

The smile disappeared from Ricco's face as he nodded with understanding.

CHAPTER TWENTY-ONE

At last Ricco gave me the word. He and Brutto had kidnapped Ivan Trotsky, Jimmy Pecan, The Generalissimo and Father Gandolfo. The whole shooting match were at the Inferno tied to chairs and awaiting my arrival, along with Frankie who was still sitting there in disbelief.

Rose was home with little Pissimo. My mother was acting like a doting grandmother, back to her old self, having gotten over her brief affair with Louie, the Groom. Marilyn was making a visit with Crayton in tow, and Little Vinnie was up in his bedroom laying in bed watching the same little spider walking across the ceiling thinking about Princess Snow Feather. At the same time, Princess Snow Feather was laying in her bedroom in Chief Panther Bob's mansion watching a little spider walk across her ceiling too thinking about Little Vinnie. The two crime bosses, Overlord Pierre, and Lazaro Salsa had rebuilt their clubs and had made peace with Chief Panther Bob who promised his daughter Princess Snow Feather would no longer be able to make war since the War Council had disbanded and were devoting their energies to putting casinos in Washington, D.C.

The Friggin' Altos
A Crime Family Gone Crazy

You'll also be happy to hear that Carmella was back home minus her Falfalla persona, because Pecan had not had the chance to run off with her because she was too busy boffing Frankie.

So most of my little family was contented and happy. Of course they had no idea what was going on at the Inferno. My own feeling was once these trials were over I would finally be able to sit down with Rose and discuss retiring to a deserted island in the Caribbean. Ivan had given me the idea. Rose was all for it.

Then it was time to go to the Inferno. I managed to stir Little Vinnie up to come with me. I thought he deserved to be in on the end of all our tribulations of which he had been a part. He had seen the wisdom of forgiving Marilyn, his adopted Aunt, and in his newfound peace of spirit welcomed her into the family.

So, we left behind us everyone we loved with the warm feeling that love and peace reined in the Alto family.

When we entered the closed-up club it was around midnight and the place was eerie in its red and black décor. It really did look like hell. I saw a huge figure sitting at the bar nursing a drink, and I sent Vinnie ahead while I had some words with Brutto Demenza.

I hadn't seen Brutto for a long time, but he was as scary as I remembered him to be. When he saw me he stood up and came to hug me. He was seven feet if he was an inch. He always wore this black wool suit with the ill-fitting pants and open front jacket over a black sweater that looked like ready-wear from a thrift shop. His movements were unsure and jerky like he really wasn't too coordinated in walking yet. His face was a huge square with a smattering of hair on top. His skin always looked like it was tinged with green, and there were two lumps, one on each side of his neck that reminded me of bolts, you know the kind that you attach electrical wires to. And believe it or not, his style of speaking was kinda grunting and his voice sounded exactly like Boris Karloff.

"Brutto," I said as I endured his hug, "it's an honor to see you again. Are you ready to play Morte o Peggiore with my guests?" His laugh boomed shaking the room and the furniture danced a little.

"My friend, Vinnie Alto, my friend. I kiss you in the name of friendship. Friendship, good—fire bad. Morte o Peggiore, fun, fun. Who I kill? I got plane to catch. Jesse waiting. Where people?"

I brought him downstairs and showed him the victims. Ricco had done a good job. They were

The Friggin' Altos
A Crime Family Gone Crazy

all tied to chairs in a neat row against the wall across the room. There had been lively conversation going on between them, until I stepped in the room with Brutto, then they all shut their mouths in fear and amazement.

"There they are Brutto in all their glory. The ones tied to the chairs. They have been very disrespectful to me. Ricco here is my Capo, and this is Little Vinnie, my son. He has a bullet lodged in his groin so don't stand in front of him cause it could come shooting out at anytime."

"Who is that over there?" Brutto grunted it out.

"Oh, so you see Al Capone too. He's going to be on our judge's panel, along with Ricco, Sammy Six Toes, and Little Vinnie."

I left him teetering and walked up to the front of the room and gave them all, what we call The Sicilian Stare: dark and menacing.

"You all know why you're here. Father Gandolfo, you are trying to interfere with my wife keeping our baby, Pissimo.

"You are the nosiest son-of-a-gun I ever saw. Something has to be done to teach you to mind your own business. Trotsky, you have betrayed me taking my wife away behind my back. Generalissimo, jeez, what can I say, you won't give me a friggin' liquor license. Pecan, I never got even for Rose's eyes, or the bullet you put in me when we were both young, or for conspiring with Marilyn to kill me and Little Vinnie. And now you want to take away Pissimo from Rose. You ain't the real father. Father Gandolfo knows who the real father is. But, Your DNA might prove your part of the real father's family and you'll take Pissimo away.

"I can't take the chance. And what's in the little box might be something in your favor. Last, but not least, is Frankie who has dishonored my pure Carmella without my permission."

"Now, Ricco here will conduct the ritual and explain the rules. Ricco, you're on."

"Thank you, Vinnie. We are going to play Morte or Peggiore. If you've never played before here are the rules. We take you one at a time and ask you a question. You may have ten minutes to give us your answer. Then we turn the decision over to our distinguished panel of judges. They, in turn, will vote, Morte or Peggiore. Death or Worse. If they vote Morte, you die. If they vote Peggiore, you get a punishment worse than death. Brutto will carry out the Morte votes. Vinnie will carry out the Peggiore votes.

Any questions?"

Trotsky the lawyer pipes up.

The Friggin' Altos
A Crime Family Gone Crazy

"What could be worse than death?"

I tell him he'll find out.

"But, what if they vote neither Morte o Peggiore?" Just like a lawyer.

"Then you will find that out if the time comes, which ain't going to happen."

I turn to Ricco. "Let's have our first contestant, Ricco."

Sammy Six Toes unties Father Gandolfo and brings him to the front of the room. He turns him over to Ricco who is standing on a little stage. I'm sitting down in front and the panel is sitting in four chairs lined up side by side to my right.

"And our first contestant is Father Peter Gandolfo. Your question is, what makes you so nosey?"

The father stands straight and rigid and looks directly at me. He ain't no shrinking violet—but then no busybody ever is.

"Vinnie, Vinnie, Vinnie. How long has it been since you've been to church? I would never allow Mr. Pecan to pretend he is Pissimo's real father. It was just that I must hear all sides as to who has rights in the matter. As unlikely as it is, he could have had blood similar to the real father. He might be a close relative on the real father's side. I had to be sure there were no other claims on the boy other than his real father and mother. I did do the test. Jimmy Pecan has no claims on little Pissimo. Only his Aunt Marilyn is the next of kin, and since she has decided to give her nephew to you and Rose to raise, the matter is settled. I will gladly give the little box to Rose to open to see if there is anything in there that cinches who his real father is. Rose must tell the boy when he is old enough to understand and I have promised Rose to tell her the father's name immediately. She has already promised to do so, so she may have whatever is in the box to give to little Pissimo as a momento. That is my answer."

Well, he's got good points on his side but there are things he has done that rub me the wrong way.

"Father Gandolfo, you are like an old woman. You stick your nose in where it doesn't belong instead of letting the people involved sort things out. Even the Bishop tells me you're a real Yenta. You interfered when I was trying to get Lacy to have an abortion. You interfered by buying my house to give Lacy a place to stay until she had the baby. You have interfered in getting blood tests and keeping secret the name of the real father and keeping the box from everyone involved. You may think your actions were the moral thing to do, but I'm not interested in the moral thing, I'm interested in what makes me happy. Because of you, I've almost lost Rose. So I turn now to our panel of judges.

How do you vote, panel, Morte o Peggiore?"
Ricco: "Peggiore."
Sammy: "Peggiore."
Al Capone: "I'ma vote baseball bat."
Little Vinnie: "Peggiore."
"Sorry, father, the vote is that you receive worse than death. My Mother Frances is a lonely crazy old broad who can't stop talking. My pal the Bishop has given you to her as her spiritual counselor, twenty-fours hour a day, seven days a week. Now what do you say?"

Father Gandolfo is crying. "Peggiore che Morte. Worse than death. I've met your mother. Please kill me."

"Brutto, put him in the holding tank. Make sure he gets to my mother."

"I watch careful. He no go no place."

"All right, Ricco. Let's continue."

"Our next contestant for Morte o Peggiore is Ivan Trotsky, Vinnie's Lawyer, stockbroker and traitor. Your question is, did you really think you could steal Rose Alto away?"

Trotsky stands tall and elegant.

"I make no excuses. I have been in love with Rose since she worked for my mother before she married Vinnie. If I had a brain I would have asked her to marry me and saved her from the likes of you, Vinnie Alto. Remember, I know everything there is to know about the Alto Empire."

"Yeah," I tell him, "that's what makes this so tricky. Well, judges, how do you vote?"

Ricco: "Peggiore."

Sammy: "Yeah, yeah, Peggiore."

Al: "I'ma vote for the baseball bat."

Little Vinnie: "Peggiore."

"You see how it is, Ivan. You get worse than death."

"No, no, not that?"

"Yep, we're sending you on a lovely trip to our organization in Russia. They'll put you to work selling numbers to the peasants in Siberia. Cold and Dark all year round is Siberia. Comrade Smirnoff says he's got a sister with a mustache. Dosvidanya, Trotsky."

Ivan puts his hands over his face.

"Worse than death. Please kill me."

Brutto comes lumbering down and takes him by the arm. "I know, holding tank. I watch."

"And now, Ricco, who's our next contestant?

The Friggin' Altos
A Crime Family Gone Crazy

"The Generalissimo. Come on down and join the fun. You're question is, why won't you give Vinnie a liquor license?"

He is tall with his blue sash and white uniform.

"I cannot allow an outsider to settle in Miami and gain power. The three crime bosses were here long before I was, but I have become all-powerful. Sunny Miami is my home. I am the most macho man in all of the world, including Peoria. The women cry for me, the men envy me my testosterone. They have made me a God—that is what I am, "El Dios." I cannot let anyone have more power than I have. You are strong Vinnie Alto, your power is as strong as mine, I cannot permit you to build more power by allowing you to settle permanently in Miami starting with your club. You must go. There can only be one El Dios."

"Guys?"

Ricco: "Peggiore."

Sammy: "Peggiore."

Al: "Forget the baseball bat, Peggiore."

Little Vinnie: "Peggiore."

"You have heard the decision of the panel. Worse than Death is their answer. From here you will be flown to freezing Alaska where the cold will freeze your Latin bones. I am sending Dickie

Blue and Tin Cup with you. You will live in an isolated cabin near the North Pole. They will guard you and see that you are kept warm."

The General shrivels in despair.

"It is too cruel—too brutal. Please, kill me."

He is led away by Brutto who is fascinated by his shiny medals.

"All right, Ricco, let's continue on."

"Our next contestant is Jimmy Pecan. Step right up Jimmy and meet your host. Your question is, "Aren't you ashamed of being such a scumbag?"

Jimmy is a broken man.

"Okay, Vinnie, you got me. Maybe I did go too far hurting Rose, shooting you years ago, and plotting to kill you and your son, Little Vinnie. But, I can say one true thing, I did love Lacy Love. I only wish Pissimo had been my son. Every man wants to leave something behind him. Remember this, maybe someday Pissimo's real father will come looking for him. Then you'll have to give him up. I don't care what you do to me now, I'd just like to be around to see that day come."

"You were always a whining, sniveling coward Pecan. When the right time comes Pissimo will know who his real father is. But, no one, will ever take that boy away from Rose. No, Jimmy, the panel doesn't have to vote. I say its Morte for you. Take him away Brutto."

Suddenly, Little Vinnie screams. "LOOK OUT! Pecan's got a gun!"

There's confusion everywhere. People are running around trying to get out of the way, footsteps running, shouting voices.

Everyone has ducked down behind the furniture. Jimmy Pecan is standing there with his gun in his hand looking for me. I was standing right out in the open across from him with my own gun raised. A perfect target. He had the drop on me all right, I was a dead man for sure. Then there is sudden silence. And then what do we hear?

We hear the sound of a shot. It rings out and a body falls down with a groan and hits the floor.

Ricco is standing shaking and pointing to a heap on the floor.

"Hey, it's Pecan. He's dead on the floor shot through the head. What happened?"

It was my turn to tell them.

"I'll tell you what happened. The bullet that was lodged in Little Vinnie's groin finally shot out his penis and shot Jimmy! He blew Jimmy's brain's out."

LaVerne and Sam Zocco

"Jimmy Buffet was right, to everything there is a season. Little Vinnie saved my life. Attitudes and latitudes."

After that we all went to take a pee and to stop shaking. They were all slapping Little Vinnie on the back, and I was so proud of my kid I hugged him and kissed him until he begged for air. When we all came back into the room we were celebrating, laughing and ready to go upstairs and have a party at an open bar. And then we all spotted Frankie still tied to the chair looking lonely and forgotten. All eyes turned to me. I knew what they were all thinking. They all wanted me to give Frankie his freedom as a thanks-be-to-God for God's mercy that we were all alive. When they saw I wasn't budging they all sat down and refused to play anymore. They were waiting for me, the boss, to be fair.

When I looked like I was going to continue the game they all sat in stone-like silence.

"Well Frankie," I said, "I guess this is it. I can see you don't need me to tell you about Morte o Peggiore or how it's played. This is your question for all the marbles. Why did you put it to my daughter Carmella? Have you so little respect for me? I took you off the streets, I gave you a job. I trusted you with all I loved by naming you my successor. And still you took her? Why? Why?

As a father I have the right to know."

Ricco stood up. "Vinnie's right, Frankie, he has the right to know."

Frankie's eyes never left my face.

"Vinnie, I used to be afraid of you and what you would do to me. I knew all the reasons you wanted to keep your little girl pure and why you didn't think I was right for her. I've tortured myself with them. I love you like my father, I owe you respect for what you did for me. She's your beloved daughter, she's my goddaughter and I should be the one who protects her from scumbags who want what I wanted. Only you can't discount this reason no more even though you would like to.

"I love her, I want to marry her, and I will always cherish her and I want to bring honor to you and Rose by asking you for her as my wife."

Ricco jumped up with tears in his eyes.

"My God, that's so beautiful. I vote Vita—Life!"

Sammy Six Toes was right behind him.

"Bravo, Frankie. I vote Vita—Life!"

"What a nicea boy," Al says, "Vita—Life and Amore—Love!"

Little Vinnie ran to Frankie and bends down and hugs him.

"Hooray for Frankie, Papa. Vita—my brother-in-law soon to be, Salute. What do you say, Papa?"

They had all been so busy watching Frankie they forgot about me. They all turn in my direction expecting my answer with shining faces of happiness. There is a big explosion!

Ricco shouted out in horror when he saw me.

"My God—Vinnie has collapsed! Look at him, he's dying. Someone call for an ambulance. Boss, oh Boss, please don't die—please don't die."

But I was already dead. The bullet that had been travelling through my system had finally hit my heart and blown it apart.

I never got the chance to vote.

I had a very nice funeral. During the ceremony at the house, Ricco came up to Rose who, like I said, was a brick.

"Rose, the ice wagon is outside. I'm sorry, I mean the Disney Cryogenics Institute truck is outside to pick up Vinnie."

"Tell them to wait. They can come in after Father Gandolfo is through with the service. Oh, and Ricco take Pissimo upstairs and change his diaper."

The Friggin' Altos
A Crime Family Gone Crazy

Ricco is muttering under his breath. "A Capo changing a diaper." He turns to Rose. "Things ain't going to be the same without the boss. Do you really think freezing him until they develop the technology to put his heart back together will work?"

Rose lets go a deep sigh.

"We can only wait and see. Oh, Frankie, did you see that Ivan Trotsky was brought back from Russia, and that the Generalisssimo, Tin Cup and Dickie Blue were given the chance to come back to Miami?"

The sad organ music is playing in the background as the newly married Frankie comes over to Rose.

"Ivan will be here any minute. Dickie Blue, Tin Cup and the General turned me down. But they sent us a photograph of them outside their cabin "El Dios," in the Klondike. The General looks the happiest of all. And look, in the picture there's this fourth guy hugging the General. On the back of the postcard it says his name is Dana the gay realtor. He ran to Alaska when the New York Police charged him with Tony Sweet's murder. Go figure."

Then Frankie looks sheepishly at Rose.

"Rose, how do you think Vinnie would have voted on my case if he had lived?" Stupid Ricco had filled Rose in on Morte o Peggiore.

"I'm sure he would have voted for vita and amore."

Just then Carmella, the new bride, calls down from upstairs to Frankie in that whiny Brooklynese voice.

"Frankie, will you get up here? I don't like being ignored. And, Oh, get me some aspirin, I feel another one of my headaches coming on tonight."

Frankie walks away and talks to the air clasping his hands in a prayer to the heavens.

"Peggiore che Morte—Worse than death."

Meanwhile Little Vinnie and Crayton are talking in the kitchen.

"Crayton, my dear friend, I release Marilyn from all debts to the Alto family for shooting me. She is free to see her nephew anytime she wants to. I carry no hard feelings."

Crayton is relieved.

"What are your plans Little Vinnie?"

"I'm all healed. I think I've talked Adam Billy, formerly Princess Snow Feather, into packing up the bong pipe, the sauna and the ugly stick and following her Big Moccasins down to the Keys.

The Friggin' Altos
A Crime Family Gone Crazy

Jimmy Buffet says the marguerites are on ice, the tropical breezes are blowing and the ocean is calling our name. By the way what are you and Marilyn going to do now?"

"I'm running for Mayor of Miami and Marilyn has promised to be my personal handler."

Little Vinnie laughs. "Finally, Dante's Inferno will get a liquor license."

Crayton is very serious and shakes his head side to side emphatically.

"No, siree. The building inspector says the place is too close to City Hall and it has to be torn down. If only Big Vinnie had built it one more foot to the South, he'd have gotten his wish. The Generalissimo was right not to give him a liquor license."

They hear a groan coming from my coffin. Little Vinnie shakes his head. "The Inferno gone." Another groan.

They both look at each other with trembling lips and tears in their eyes. About time.

"Will we ever see another Vinnie Alto?" My son asks his friend the million-dollar question while they shake hands.

"That's the million dollar question. Will he ever come back?"

LaVerne and Sam Zocco

Meanwhile Rose is talking to Father Gandolfo in front of my beautiful casket.

"Father Gandolfo, you wanted to see me? It was a beautiful service—Vinnie would have loved it."

"We have unfinished business, Rose. Quick before Frances comes looking for me. I asked Frankie to be here to witness our meeting."

From the hall comes my mother's grinding voice.

"Hey Gandolfo, are you ready to go?"

The father is looking jumpy and nervous.

"I wanted to tell you who the real father of Pissimo is so you can tell him when he grows up. Here is the box he gave to Lacy when she first knew she was pregnant."

"Hey, Gandolfo." By now my mother is shrieking.

Father Gandolfo throws the box to Rose. "Good-bye and God bless you." He runs out the door.

"I'm a little nervous Frankie. Will you help me open this box?" So they open the box right in front of my coffin.

"Well, I'll be," says Frankie. "Look, it's a pair of baby shoes made out of snakeskin!! They match the ones Tony Sweets used to wear all the time. Jeez, Tony Sweets is the father of Pissimo."

Right then and there I let out another moan from inside the casket.

"Frankie, did you hear that. I thought it came from—no, it couldn't be."

That's when the icemen come in and took me and my casket off to the icehouse.

Then I hear those sweet Italian tones.

"Jeez, Vinnie, can you move over, it's crowded down here by your feet." It's Al. What a guy.

THE END

ABOUT THE AUTHOR

LaVerne and Sam Zocco are a mother and son team who think the premise of an inept mafia crime family is hilarious and fits right in with the humor that is always a part of their Sicilian family.

Sam, in his day job, is the Director of a Substance Abuse Center called, "Here's Help, Inc. LaVerne has come to writing late in life but has a busy life as an author and Mental Health Counselor.

The Friggin' Altos ran as a radio program in serial form on Y-100 in South Florida. Each episode was one minute a day, five days a week. It was a popular, quirky program that built a following for this insane crime family. Written by LaVerne and promoted by Sam with all his good suggestions, the book just came naturally.

LaVerne and Sam both live in Pembroke Pines, Fla. Sam lives with his lovely wife, Kim, who is a teacher, and their children, Sal and Tayler. LaVerne has a son, younger than Sam, John L. Zocco, Jr. who troubleshoots for the post Office and lives in Hollywood, Florida.

Breinigsville, PA USA
13 July 2010
241751BV00001B/4/A